I0575276

John Boyle O'Reilly

Songs, Legends, and Ballads

John Boyle O'Reilly

Songs, Legends, and Ballads

ISBN/EAN: 9783744778237

Printed in Europe, USA, Canada, Australia, Japan

Cover: Foto ©Andreas Hilbeck / pixelio.de

More available books at **www.hansebooks.com**

SONGS,

LEGENDS AND BALLADS.

BY

JOHN BOYLE O'REILLY.

SEVENTH EDITION.

BOSTON:
THE PILOT PUBLISHING COMPANY.
1890.

COPYRIGHT, 1880,
BY JOHN BOYLE O'REILLY.

TO

My Dear Wife,

WHOSE RARE AND LOVING JUDGMENT HAS BEEN A STANDARD

I HAVE TRIED TO REACH,

I DEDICATE THIS BOOK.

SONGS, LEGENDS, AND BALLADS.

CONTENTS.

viii CONTENTS.

THE RAINBOW'S TREASURE.

WHERE the foot of the rainbow meets the
    field,
  And the grass resplendent glows,
The earth will a precious treasure yield,
  So the olden story goes.
In a crystal cup are the diamonds piled
  For him who can swiftly chase
Over torrent and desert and precipice wild,
  To the rainbow's wandering base.

There were two in the field at work, one day,
  Two brothers, who blithely sung,
When across their valley's deep-winding way
  The glorious arch was flung!

And one saw naught but a sign of rain,
   And feared for his sheaves unbound;
And one is away, over mountain and plain,
   Till the mystical treasure is found!

Through forest and stream, in a blissful dream,
   The rainbow lured him on;
With a siren's guile it loitered awhile,
   Then leagues away was gone.
Over brake and brier he followed fleet;
   The people scoffed as he passed;
But in thirst and heat, and with wounded feet,
   He nears the prize at last.

It is closer and closer — he wins the race —
   One strain for the goal in sight:
Its radiance falls on his yearning face —
   The blended colors unite!
He laves his brow in the iris beam —
   He reaches —— Ah woe! the sound
From the misty gulf where he ends his dream,
   And the crystal cup is found!

'Tis the old, old story : one man will read
   His lesson of toil in the sky ;
While another is blind to the present need,
   But sees with the spirit's eye.
You may grind their souls in the self-same mill,
   You may bind them, heart and brow ;
But the poet will follow the rainbow still,
   And his brother will follow the plough.

AT BEST.

THE faithful helm commands the keel,
   From port to port fair breezes blow ;
But the ship must sail the convex sea,
   Nor may she straighter go.

So, man to man ; in fair accord,
   On thought and will, the winds may wait ;
But the world will bend the passing word,
   Though its shortest course be straight.

From soul to soul the shortest line
　At best will bended be :
The ship that holds the straightest course
　Still sails the convex sea.

MACARIUS THE MONK.

IN the old days, while yet the Church was
　　young,
And men believed that praise of God was sung
In curbing self as well as singing psalms,
There lived a monk, Macarius by name,
A holy man, to whom the faithful came
With hungry hearts to hear the wondrous Word.
In sight of gushing springs and sheltering palms,
He dwelt within the desert : from the marsh
He drank the brackish water, and his food
Was dates and roots,— and all his rule was harsh,
For pampered flesh in those days warred with
　　good.

From those who came in scores a few there were
Who feared the devil more than fast and prayer,
And these remained and took the hermit's vow.
A dozen saints there grew to be ; and now
Macarius, happy, lived in larger care.
He taught his brethren all the lore he knew,
And as they learned, his pious rigors grew.
His whole intent was on the spirit's goal :
He taught them silence — words disturb the soul :
He warned of joys, and bade them pray for
    sorrow,
And be prepared to-day for death to-morrow
To know that human life alone was given
To prove the souls of those who merit heaven ;
He bade the twelve in all things be as brothers,
And die to self, to live and work for others.
" For so," he said, " we save our love and labors,
And each one gives his own and takes his
    neighbor's."

Thus long he taught, and while they silent heard,
He prayed for fruitful soil to hold the Word.

One day, beside the marsh they labored long,—
For worldly work makes sweeter sacred song,—
And when the cruel sun made hot the sand,
And Afric's gnats the sweltering face and hand
Tormenting stung, a passing traveller stood
And watched the workers by the reeking flood.
Macarius, nigh, with heat and toil was faint;
The traveller saw, and to the suffering saint
A bunch of luscious grapes in pity threw.
Most sweet and fresh and fair they were to view,
A generous cluster, bursting-rich with wine.
Macarius longed to taste. "The fruit is mine,"
He said, and sighed; "but I, who daily teach,
Feel now the bond to practise as I preach."
He gave the cluster to the nearest one,
And with his heavy toil went patient on.

As one athirst will greet a flowing brim,
The tempting fruit made moist the mouth of him
Who took the gift; but in the yearning eye
Rose brighter light: to one whose lip was dry
He gave the grapes, and bent him to his spade.

And he who took, unknown to any other,
The sweet refreshment handed to a brother.
And so, from each to each, till round was made
The circuit wholly — when the grapes at last,
Untouched and tempting, to Macarius passed.

"Now God be thanked!" he cried, and ceased his
    toil;
"The seed was good, but better was the soil.
My brothers, join with me to bless the day."
But, ere they knelt, he threw the grapes away.

THE TRIAL OF THE GODS.

"On a regular division of the [Roman] Senate, Jupiter was
condemned and degraded by the sense of a very large major-
ity." — *Gibbon's Decline and Fall.*

NEVER nobler was the Senate,
   Never grander the debate:
Rome's old gods are on their trial
   By the judges of the state!

Torn by warring creeds, the Fathers
   Urge to-day the question home —
" Whether Jupiter or Jesus
   Shall be God henceforth in Rome?"

Lo, the scene! In Jove's own temple,
   As of old, the Fathers meet;
Through the porch, to hear the speeches,
   Press the people from the street.
Pontiffs, rich with purple vesture,
   Pass from senate chair to chair;
Learnéd augurs, still as statues —
   Voiceless statues, too — are there;
Vestal virgins, white with terror,
   Mutely asking — what has come?
What new light shall turn to darkness
   Vesta's holy fire in Rome?

Answer, Quindecemvirs! Surely,
   Of this wondrous Nazarene
Ye must know, who keep the secrets
   Of the prophet Sibylline?

Nay, no word! Here stand the Flamens :
    Have ye read the omens, priests?
Slain the victims, white and sable,
    Scanned the entrails of the beasts?

Priest of Pallas, see! the people
    Ask for oracles to-day :
Silent! Priests of Mars and Venus?
    Lo, they turn, dumb-lipped, away!
Priest of Jove? Flamen dialis!
    Here in Jove's own temple meet
In debate the Roman Senate,
    And Jove's priest with timid feet
Stands beyond the altar railing!
    Gods, I feel ye frown above!
In the shadow of Jove's altar
    Men defy the might of Jove!

Treason riots in the temple
    At the sacrilege profound :
Virgins mocked, and augurs banished,
    And divinities discrowned!

Hush!   Old Rome herself appeareth,
　　Pleading for the ancient faith :
Urging all her by-gone glory —
　　That to change the old were death.
Rudely answer the patricians,
　　Scoffing at the time-worn snare :
Twice a thousand years of sacrifice
　　Have melted into air ;
Twice a thousand years of worship
　　Have bitterly sufficed
To prove there is no Jupiter !
　　The Senate votes for Christ !

———

Not aimless is the story,
　　The moral not remote :
For still the gods are questioned,
　　And still the Senates vote.
Men sacrifice to Venus ;
　　To Mars are victims led ;
And Mercury is honored still ;
　　And Bacchus is not dead ; —

But these are minor deities
    That cling to human sight :
Our twilight they — but Right and Wrong
    Are clear as day and night.
We know the Truth : but falsehood
    With our lives is so inwove —
Our Senates vote down Jesus
    As old Rome degraded Jove !

———

THE SHADOW.

THERE is a shadow on the sunny wall,
    Dark and forbidding, like a bode of ill ;
Go, drive it thence.   Alas, such shadows fall
    From real things, nor may be moved at will.

There is a shadow on my heart to-day,
    A cloudy grief condensing to a tear :
Alas, I cannot drive its gloom away —
    Some sin or sorrow casts the shapeless fear.

THE VALUE OF GOLD.

THERE may be standard weight for precious
    metal,
  But deeper meaning it must ever hold;
Thank God, there are some things no law can settle,
  And one of these — the real worth of gold.

The stamp of king or crown has common power
  To hold the traffic-value in control;
Our coarser senses note this worth — the lower;
  The higher comes from senses of the soul.

This truth we find not in mere warehouse learning—
  The value varies with the hands that hold;
The worth depends upon the mode of earning;
  And this man's copper equals that man's gold.

With empty heart, and forehead lined with
    scheming,
  Men's sin and sorrow have been that man's gain;

But this man's heart, with rich emotions teeming,
    Makes fine the gold for which he coins his brain.

But richer still than gold from upright labor —
    The only gold that should have standard price—
Is the poor earning of our humble neighbor,
    Whose every coin is red with sacrifice.

Mere store of money is not wealth, but rather
    The proof of poverty and need of bread.
Like men themselves is the bright gold they gather ·
    It may be living, or it may be dead.

It may be filled with love and life and vigor,
    To guide the wearer, and to cheer the way;
It may be corpse-like in its weight and rigor,
    Bending the bearer to his native clay.

There is no comfort but in outward showing
    In all the servile homage paid to dross;
Better to heart and soul the silent knowing
    Our little store has not been gained by loss.

PEACE AND PAIN.

THE day and night are symbols of creation,
　　And each has part in all that God has made;
There is no ill without its compensation,
　　And life and death are only light and shade.
There never beat a heart so base and sordid
　　But felt at times a sympathetic glow;
There never lived a virtue unrewarded,
　　Nor died a vice without its meed of woe.

In this brief life despair should never reach us;
　　The sea looks wide because the shores are dim;
The star that led the Magi still can teach us
　　The way to go if we but look to Him.
And as we wade, the darkness closing o'er us,
　　The hungry waters surging to the chin,
Our deeds will rise like stepping-stones before us —
　　The good and bad — for we may use the sin.

A sin of youth, atoned for and forgiven,
   Takes on a virtue, if we choose to find :
When clouds across our onward path are driven,
   We still may steer by its pale light behind.
A sin forgotten is in part to pay for,
   A sin remembered is a constant gain :
Sorrow, next joy, is what we ought to pray for,
   As next to peace we profit most from pain.

A SEED.

A KINDLY act is a kernel sown,
   That will grow to a goodly tree,
Shedding its fruit when time has flown
   Down the gulf of eternity.

CHUNDER ALI'S WIFE.

FROM THE HINDOSTANEE.

"I AM poor," said Chunder Ali, while the Man-
        darin above him
Frowned in supercilious anger at the dog who
        dared to speak;
"I am friendless and a Hindoo: such a one meets
        few to love him
Here in China, where the Hindoo finds the truth
        alone is weak.
I have naught to buy your justice; were I wise, I
        had not striven.
Speak your judgment;" and he crossed his arms
        and bent his quivering face.

Heard he then the unjust sentence: all his goods
    and gold were given
To another, and he stood alone, a beggar in the
    place.

And the man who bought the judgment looked
    in triumph and derision
At the cheated Hindoo merchant, as he rubbed
    his hands and smiled
At the whispered gratulation of his friends, and at
    the vision
Of the more than queenly dower for Ahmeer, his
    only child.
Fair Ahmeer, who of God's creatures was the only
    one who loved him,
She, the diamond of his treasures, the one lamb
    within his fold,
She, whose voice, like her dead mother's, was the
    only power that moved him, —
She would praise the skill that gained her all this
    Hindoo's silk and gold.
And the old man thanked Confucius, and the judge,
    and him who pleaded.

But why falls this sudden silence ? why does each
    one hold his breath ?
Every eye turns on the Hindoo, who before was
    all unheeded,
And in wond'ring expectation all the court grows
    still as death.

Not alone stood Chunder Ali : by his side Ahmeer
    was standing,
And his brown hand rested lightly on her shoulder
    as he smiled
At the sweet young face turned toward him. Then
    the father's voice commanding
Fiercely bade his daughter to him from the dog
    whose touch defiled.
But she moved not, and she looked not at her father
    or the others
As she answered, with her eyes upon the Hindoo's
    noble face :
" Nay, my father, he defiles not : this kind arm above
    all others
Is my choosing, and forever by his side shall be my
    place.

When you knew not, his dear hand had given
    many a sweet love-token,
He had gathered all my heartstrings and had
    bound them round his life ;
Yet you tell me he defiles me ; nay, my father,
    you have spoken
In your anger, and not knowing I was Chunder
    Ali's wife."

A KISS.

LOVE is a plant with double root,
    And of strange, elastic power :
Men's minds are divided in naming the fruit,
    But a kiss is only the flower.

BONE AND SINEW AND BRAIN.

YE white-maned waves of the Western Sea.
   That ride and roll to the strand,
Ye strong-winged birds, never forced a-lee
   By the gales that sweep toward land,
Ye are symbols of death, and of hope that saves,
   As ye swoop in your strength and grace,
As ye roll to the land like the billowed graves
   Of a past and puerile race.

Cry, " Presto, change ! " and the lout is lord,
   With his vulgar blood turned blue ;
Go dub your knight with a slap of a sword,
   As the kings in Europe do ;
Go grade the lines of your social mode
   As you grade the palace wall,—
The people forever to bear the load,
   And the gilded vanes o'er all.

But the human blocks will not lie as still
    As the dull foundation-stones,
But will rise, like a sea, with an awful will,
    And ingulf the golden thrones;
For the days are gone when a special race
    Took the place of the gilded vane;
And the merit that mounts to the highest place
    Must have bone and sinew and brain.

Let the cant of "the march of mind" be heard,
    Of the time to come, when man
Shall lose the mark of his brawn and beard
    In the future's levelling plan:
'Tis the dream of a mind effeminate,
    The whine for an easy crown;
There is no meed for the good and great
    In the weakling's levelling down.

A nation's boast is a nation's bone,
    As well as its might of mind;
And the culture of either of these alone
    Is the doom of a nation signed.

But the cant of the ultra-suasion school
   Unsinews the hand and thigh,
And preaches the creed of the weak to rule,
   And the strong to struggle and die.
Our schools are spurred to the fatal race,
   As if health were the nation's sin,
Till the head grows large, and the vampire face
   Is gorged on the limbs so thin.
Our women have entered the abstract fields,
   And avaunt with the child and home:
While the rind of science a pleasure yields
   Shall they care for the lives to come?
And they ape the manners of manly times
   In their sterile and worthless life,
Till the man of the future augments his crimes
   With a raid for a Sabine wife.

Ho, white-maned waves of the Western Sea,
   That ride and roll to the strand!
Ho, strong-winged birds, never blown a-lee
   By the gales that sweep toward land!

Ye are symbols both of a hope that saves,
   As ye swoop in your strength and grace,
As ye roll to the land like the billowed graves
   Of a suicidal race.
Ye have hoarded your strength in equal parts;
   For the men of the future reign
Must have faithful souls and kindly hearts,
   And bone and sinew and brain.

TO-DAY.

ONLY from day to day
   The life of a wise man runs;
What matter if seasons far away
   Have gloom or have double suns?

To climb the unreal path,
   We stray from the roadway here;
We swim the rivers of wrath,
   And tunnel the hills of fear.

Our feet on the torrent's brink,
  Our eyes on the cloud afar,
We fear the things we think,
  Instead of the things that are.

Like a tide our work should rise —
  Each later wave the best;
To-day is a king in disguise,*
  To-day is the special test.

Like a sawyer's work is life:
  The present makes the flaw,
And the only field for strife
  Is the inch before the saw.

---

* "The days are ever divine. . . . . They come and go like muffled and veiled figures, sent from a distant friendly party; but they say nothing; and if we do not use the gifts they bring, they carry them as silently away."—*Emerson*.

MY NATIVE LAND.

IT chanced to me upon a time to sail
   Across the Southern Ocean to and fro;
And, landing at fair isles, by stream and vale
   Of sensuous blessing did we ofttimes go.
And months of dreamy joys, like joys in sleep,
   Or like a clear, calm stream o'er mossy stone,
Unnoted passed our hearts with voiceless sweep,
   And left us yearning still for lands unknown.

And when we found one, — for 'tis soon to find
   In thousand-isled Cathay another isle, —
For one short noon its treasures filled the mind,
   And then again we yearned, and ceased to smile.
And so it was, from isle to isle we passed,
   Like wanton bees or boys on flowers or lips;

And when that all was tasted. then at last
 We thirsted still for draughts instead of sips.

I learned from this there is no Southern land
 Can fill with love the hearts of Northern men.
Sick minds need change ; but, when in health they
  stand
 'Neath foreign skies, their love flies home agen.
And thus with me it was : the yearning turned
 From laden airs of cinnamon away,
And stretched far westward, while the full heart
  burned
 With love for Ireland, looking on Cathay!

My first dear love, all dearer for thy grief!
 My land, that has no peer in all the sea
For verdure, vale, or river, flower or leaf, —
 If first to no man else, thou 'rt first to me.
New loves may come with duties, but the first
 Is deepest yet, — the mother's breath and smiles :
Like that kind face and breast where I was nursed
 Is my poor land, the Niobe of isles.

THERE IS BLOOD ON THE EARTH.

THERE is blood on the face of the earth —
　　It reeks through the years, and is red :
Where Truth was slaughtered at birth,　.
　　And the veins of Liberty bled.

Lo ! vain is the hand that tries
　　To cover the crimson stain :
It spreads like a plague, and cries·
　　Like a soul in writhing pain.

It wasteth the planet's flesh ;
　　It calleth on breasts of stone :
God holdeth His wrath in a leash
　　Till the hearts of men atone.

Blind, like the creatures of time ;
　　Curséd, like all the race,

They answer: "The blood and crime
   Belong to a sect and place!"

What are these things to Heaven —
   Races or places of men?
The world through one Christ was forgiven —
   Nor question of races then.

The wrong of to-day shall be rued
   In a thousand coming years;
The debt must be paid in blood,
   The interest, in tears.

Shall none stand up for right
   Whom the evil passes by?
But God has the globe in sight,
   And hearkens the weak ones' cry.

Wherever a principle dies —
   Nay, principles never die!
But wherever a ruler lies,
   And a people share the lie;

Where right is crushed by force,
    And manhood is stricken dead —
There dwelleth the ancient curse,
    And the blood on the earth is red !

————

THE RIDE OF COLLINS GRAVES.

AN INCIDENT OF THE FLOOD IN MASSACHUSETTS, ON MAY 16, 1874.

NO song of a soldier riding down
    To the raging fight from Winchester town ;
No song of a time that shook the earth
With the nations' throe at a nation's birth ;
But the song of a brave man, free from fear
As Sheridan's self or Paul Revere ;
Who risked what they risked, free from strife,
And its promise of glorious pay — his life !

The peaceful valley has waked and stirred,
And the answering echoes of life are heard :

The dew still clings to the trees and grass,
And the early toilers smiling pass,
As they glance aside at the white-walled homes,
Or up the valley, where merrily comes
The brook that sparkles in diamond rills
As the sun comes over the Hampshire hills.

What was it, that passed like an ominous breath —
Like a shiver of fear, or a touch of death?
What was it?   The valley is peaceful still,
And the leaves are afire on top of the hill.
It was not a sound — nor a thing of sense —
But a pain, like the pang of the short suspense
That thrills the being of those who see
At their feet the gulf of Eternity !

The air of the valley has felt the chill :
The workers pause at the door of the mill ;
The housewife, keen to the shivering air,
Arrests her foot on the cottage stair,
Instinctive taught by the mother-love,
And thinks of the sleeping ones above.

Why start the listeners? Why does the course
Of the mill-stream widen? Is it a horse —
Hark to the sound of his hoofs, they say —
That gallops so wildly Williamsburg way!

God! what was that, like a human shriek
From the winding valley? Will nobody speak?
Will nobody answer those women who cry
As the awful warnings thunder by?

Whence come they? Listen! And now they
    hear
The sound of the galloping horse-hoofs near;
They watch the trend of the vale, and see
The rider who thunders so menacingly,
With waving arms and warning scream
To the home-filled banks of the valley stream.
He draws no rein, but he shakes the street
With a shout and the ring of the galloping feet;
And this the cry he flings to the wind:
"To the hills for your lives! The flood is
    behind!"

He cries and is gone; but they know the worst --.
The breast of the Williamsburg dam has burst!
The basin that nourished their happy homes
Is changed to a demon — It comes! it comes!

A monster in aspect, with shaggy front
Of shattered dwellings, to take the brunt
Of the homes they shatter — white-maned and
      hoarse,
The merciless Terror fills the course
Of the narrow valley, and rushing raves,
With Death on the first of its hissing waves,
Till cottage and street and crowded mill
Are crumbled and crushed.

                    But onward still,
In front of the roaring flood is heard
The galloping horse and the warning word.
Thank God! the brave man's life is spared!
From Williamsburg town he nobly dared
To race with the flood and take the road
In front of the terrible swath it mowed.

For miles it thundered and crashed behind,
But he looked ahead with a steadfast mind;
"They must be warned!" was all he said,
As away on his terrible ride he sped.

When heroes are called for, bring the crown
To this Yankee rider: send him down
On the stream of time with the Curtius old;
His deed as the Roman's was brave and bold,
And the tale can as noble a thrill awake,
For he offered his life for the people's sake.

STAR-GAZING.

LET be what is: why should we strive and
    wrestle
  With awkward skill against a subtle doubt?
Or pin a mystery 'neath our puny pestle,
  And vainly try to bray its secret out?

What boots it me to gaze at other planets,
    And speculate on sensate beings there?
It comforts not that, since the moon began its
    Well-ordered course, it knew no breath of air.

There may be men and women up in Venus,
    Where science finds both · summer-green and
        snow;
But are we happier asking, "Have they seen us?
    And, like us earth-men, do they yearn to
        know?"

On greater globes than ours men may be greater,
    For all things here in fair proportion run;
But will it make our poor cup any sweeter
    To think a nobler Shakespeare thrills the sun?

Or, that our sun is but itself a minor,
    Like this dark earth — a tenth-rate satellite,
That swings submissive round an orb diviner,
    Whose day is lightning, with our day for
        night?

Or, past all suns, to find the awful centre
    Round which they meanly wind a servile road;
Ah, will it raise us or degrade, to enter
    Where that world's Shakespeare towers almost
        to God?

No, no; far better, "lords of all creation"
    To strut our ant-hill, and to take our ease;
To look aloft and say, "That constellation
    Was lighted there our regal sight to please!"

We owe no thanks to so-called men of science,
    Who demonstrate that earth, not sun, goes
        round:
'Twere better think the sun a mere appliance
    To light man's villages and heat his ground.

There seems no good in asking or in humbling;
    The mind incurious has the most of rest;
If we can live and laugh and pray, not grum-
    bling,
    'Tis all we can do here — and 'tis the best.

The throbbing brain will burst its tender raiment
　With futile force, to see by finite light
How man's brief earning and eternal payment
　Are weighed as equal in th' Infinite sight.

'Tis all in vain to struggle with abstraction —
　The milky-way that tempts our mental glass;
The study for mankind is earth-born action;
　The highest wisdom, let the wondering pass.

The Lord knows best: He gave us thirst for
　. learning;
And deepest knowledge of His work betrays
No thirst left waterless.　Shall our soul-yearning,
　Apart from all things, be a quenchless blaze?

DOLORES.

IS he well blest who has no eyes to scan
 The woful things that shadow all our life :
The latent brute behind the eyes of man,
 The place and power gained and stained by
  strife,
 The weakly victims driven to the wall,
 The subtile cruelties that meet us all
 Like eyes from darksome places? Blest is he
 Who such sad things is never doomed to see !

The crust of common life is worn by time,
And shines deception, as a thin veneer
The raw plank hides, or as the frozen mere
Holds drownéd men embedded in its slime ;
The ninety eat their bread of death and crime,
And sin and sorrow that the ten may thrive.

O, moaning sea of life ! the few who dive
Beneath thy waters, faint and short of breath,

Not Dante-like, who cannot swim in death
And view its secrets, but must swiftly rise, —
They meet the light with introverted eyes,
And hands that clutch a few dim mysteries!

Our life a harp is, with unnumbered strings,
    And tones and symphonies; but our poor skill
Some shallow notes from its great music brings.
    We know it there; but vainly wish and will.

O, things symbolic! Things that mock our
    sense —
Our five-fold, pitiable sense — and say
A thousand senses could not show one day
As sight infinite sees it; fruitful clay,
And budding bough, and nature great with child
And chill with doom and death — is all so dense
That our dull thought can never read thy words,
Or sweep with knowing hand thy hidden chords?

Have men not fallen from fair heights, once trod
By nobler minds, who saw the works of God,

The flowers and living things, still undefiled,
And spoke one language with them? And can we,
In countless generations, each more pure
Than that preceding, come at last to see
Thy symbols full of meaning, and be sure
That what we read is all they have to tell?

———

LOVE, AND BE WISE.

NOT on the word alone
    Let love depend;
Neither by actions done
    Choose ye the friend.

Let the slow years fly —
    These are the test;
Never to peering eye
    Opened the breast.

Psyche won hopeless woe,
  Reaching to take ;
Wait till your lilies grow
  Up from the lake.

Gather words patiently ;
  Harvest the deed ;
Let the winged years fly,
  Sifting the seed.

Judging by harmony,
  Learning by strife ;
Seeking in unity
  Precept and life.

Seize the supernal —
  Prometheus dies ;
Take the external
  On trust — and be wise.

RESURGITE! — JUNE, 1877.

NOW, for the faith that is in ye,
　　Polander, Sclav, and Kelt!
Prove to the world what the lips have hurled
　The hearts have grandly felt.

Rouse, ye races in shackles!
　　See in the East, the glare
Is red in the sky, and the warning cry
　　Is sounding — "Awake! Prepare!"

A voice from the spheres — a hand downreached
　To hands that would be free,
To rend the gyves from the fettered lives
　That strain toward Liberty!

Circassia! the cup is flowing
　That holdeth perennial youth:

Who strikes succeeds, for when manhood bleeds
  Each drop is a Cadmus' tooth.

Sclavonia! first from the sheathing
  Thy knife to the cord that binds;
Thy one-tongued host shall renew the boast:
  "The Scythians are the Winds!"

Greece! to the grasp of heroes,
  Flashed with thine ancient pride,
Thy swords advance: in the passing chance
  The great of heart are tried.

Poland! thy lance-heads brighten:
  The Tartar has swept thy name
From the schoolman's chart, but the patriot's heart
  Preserves its lines in flame.

Ireland! mother of dolors,
  The trial on thee descends:
Who quaileth in fear when the test is near,
  His bondage never ends.

Oppression, that kills the craven,
   Defied, is the freeman's good :
No cause can be lost forever whose cost
   Is coined from Freedom's blood !

Liberty's wine and altar
   Are blood and human right ;
Her weak shall be strong while the struggle with
      wrong
   Is a sacrificial fight.

Earth for the people — their laws their own —
   An equal race for all :
Though shattered and few who to this are true
   Shall flourish the more they fall.

RULES OF THE ROAD.

WHAT man would be wise, let him drink of
    the river
That bears on its bosom the record of time :
A message to him every wave can deliver
    To teach him to creep till he knows how to
    climb.
Who heeds not experience, trust him not; tell
    him
    The scope of one mind can but trifles achieve :
The weakest who draws from the mine will excel
    him —
    The wealth of mankind is the wisdom they
    leave.

For peace do not hope — to be just you must
    break it ;
    Still work for the minute and not for the year ;
When honor comes to you, be ready to take it ;
    But reach not to seize it before it is near.

Be silent and safe — silence never betrays you;
  Be true to your word and your work and your
    friend;
Put least trust in him who is foremost to praise
  you,
  Nor judge of a road till it draw to the end.

Stand erect in the vale, nor exult on the moun-
  tain;
  Take gifts with a sigh — most men give to be
    paid;
"1 had" is a heartache, "I have" is a fountain,—
  You're worth what you saved, not the million
    you made.
Trust toil not intent, or your plans will miscarry;
  Your wife keep a sweetheart, instead of a
    tease;
Rule children by reason, not rod; and, mind,
  marry
  Your girl when you can — and your boy when
    you please.

Steer straight as the wind will allow; but be
  ready
To veer just a point to let travellers pass:
Each sees his own star — a stiff course is too
  steady
When this one to Meeting goes, that one to
  Mass.
Our stream's not so wide but two arches may
  span it —
Good neighbor and citizen; these for a code,
And this truth in sight,— every man on the planet
  Has just as much right as yourself to the road.

––––––

FOREVER.

THOSE we love truly never die,
  Though year by year the sad memorial
    wreath,
A ring and flowers, types of life and death,
  Are laid upon their graves.

For death the pure life saves,
And life all pure is love; and love can reach
From heaven to earth, and nobler lessons teach
Than those by mortals read.

Well blest is he who has a dear one dead:
A friend he has whose face will never change —
A dear communion that will not grow strange;
The anchor of a love is death.

The blessed sweetness of a loving breath
Will reach our cheek all fresh through weary
    years.
For her who died long since, ah! waste not
    tears,
She's thine unto the end.

Thank God for one dead friend,
With face still radiant with the light of truth,
Whose love comes laden with the scent of youth,
Through twenty years of death.

THE LOVING CUP OF THE PAPYRUS. *

WISE men use days as husbandmen use bees,
    And steal rich drops from every pregnant
      hour ;
Others, like wasps on blossomed apple-trees,
    Find gall, not honey, in the sweetest flower.

Congratulations for a scene like this !
    The olden times are here — these shall be olden
When, years to come, remembering present bliss,
    We sigh for past Papyrian dinners golden.

We thank the gods ! we call them back to light —
    Call back to hoary Egypt for Osiris,
Who first made wine, to join our board to-night,
    And drain this loving cup with the Papyrus.

---

* On February 3d, 1877, at the dinner of "The Papyrus,"
a club composed of literary men and artists of Boston, a beautiful crystal "Loving Cup" was presented to the club by Mr.
Wm. A. Hovey.

He comes! the Pharaoh's god! fling wide the
　　door —
Welcome, Osiris! See — thine old prescription
Is honored here; and thou shalt drink once more
　　With men whose treasured ensign is Egyptian.

A toast! a toast! our guest shall give a toast!
　　By Nilus' flood, we pray thee, god, inspire us!
He smiles — he wills — let not a word be lost —
　　His hand upon the cup, he speaks : —

　　　　　　　　　" PAPYRUS !

" I greet ye! and mine ancient nation shares
　　In greeting fair from Ammon, Ptah, and Isis,
Whose leaf ye love — dead Egypt's leaf, that bears
　　Our tale of pride from Cheops to Cambyses.

" We gods of Egypt, who are wise with age —
　　Five thousand years have washed us clean of
　　　　passion —   .
A golden era for this board presage,
　　While ye do keep this cup in priestly fashion.

"We love to see the bonds of fellowship
   Made still more sacred by a fine tradition;
We bless this bowl that moves from lip to lip
   In love's festoons, renewed by every mission.

"Intern the vessel from profaning eyes;
   The lip that kisses should have special merit;
Thus every sanguine draught shall symbolize
   And consecrate the true Papyrian spirit.

"For brotherhood, not wine, this cup should pass;
   Its depths should ne'er reflect the eye of malice;
Drink toasts to strangers with the social glass,
   But drink to brothers with this loving chalice.

"And now, Papyrus, each one pledge to each:
   And let this formal tie be warmly cherished.
No words are needed for a kindly speech —
   The loving thought will live when words have
      perished."

THE TREASURE OF ABRAM.

I.

IN the old Rabbinical stories,
  So old they might well be true,—
The sacred tales of the Talmud,
  That David and Solomon knew,—
There is one of the Father Abram,
  The greatest of Heber's race,
The mustard-seed of Judea
  That filled the holy place.
'Tis said that the fiery heaven
  His eye was first to read,
Till planets were gods no longer,
  But helps for the human need ;
He taught his simple people
  The scope of eternal law
That swayed at once the fleecy cloud
  And the circling suns they saw.

But the rude Chaldean peasants
  Uprose against the seer,
And drave him forth — else never came
  This Talmud legend here.

With Sarah his wife, and his servants,
  Whom he ruled with potent hand,
The Patriarch planted his vineyards
  In the Canaanitish land ;
With his wife — the sterile, but lovely,
  The fame of whose beauty grew
Till there was no land in Asia
  But tales of the treasure knew.
In his lore the sage lived — learning
  High thought from the starlit skies ;
But heedful, too, of the light at home,
  And the danger of wistful eyes ;
Till the famine fell on his corn-fields,
  And sent him forth again,
To seek for a home in Egypt,—
  The land of the amorous men.

II.

Long and rich is the caravan that halts at Egypt's
    gate,
While duty full the stranger pays on lowing herd
    and freight.
Full keen the scrutiny of those who note the
    heavy dues ;
From weanling foal to cumbrous wain, no chance
    of gain they lose.

But fair the search — no wealth concealed ; while
    rich the gifts they take
From Abram's hand, till care has ceased, and for-
    mal quest they make.
They pass the droves and laden teams, the
    weighted slaves are past,
And Abram doubles still the gifts ; one wain —
    his own — is last—
It goes unsearched ! Wise Abram smiles, though
    dearly stemmed the quest ;

But haps will come from causes slight,
And hidden things upspring to light:
A breeze flings wide the canvas fold, and deep
    within the wain, behold
A brass-bound, massive chest!

"Press on!" shouts Abram. "Hold!" they cry;
    "what treasure hide ye here?"
The word is stern—the answer brief: "Treasure!
    'tis household gear;
Plain linen cloth and flaxen thread." The
    scribes deceived are wroth;
"Then weigh the chest—its price shall be the
    dues on linen cloth!"

The face of Abram seemed to grieve, though joy
    was in his breast,
As carefully his servants took and weighed the
    mighty chest.
But one hath watched the secret smile; he
    cries—"This stranger old
Hath used deceit: no cloth is here—this chest is
    filled with gold!"

"Nay, nay," wise Abram says, and smiles, though
    now he hides dismay ;
"But time is gold : let pass the chest — on gold
    the dues I pay ! "

But he who read the subtle smile detects the se-
    cret fear :
"Detain the chest ! nor cloth nor gold, but
    precious silk is here ! "

Grave Father Abram stands like one who
    knoweth well the sword
When tyros baffle thrust and guard ; slow comes
    the heedful word :
"I seek no lawless gain — behold ! my trains
    are on their way,
Else would these bands my servants break, and
    show the simple goods I take,
That silk ye call ; but, for time's sake, on silk the
    dues I pay ! "

"He pays too much ! " the watcher cries ; "this
    man is full of guile ;

From cloth to gold and gold to silk, to save a
    paltry mile !
This graybeard pay full silken dues on cloth for
    slave-bred girls !
Some prize is here — he shall not pass until he
    pay for pearls ! "

Stern Abram turned a lurid eye, as he the man
    would slay ;
An instant, rose the self-command ; but thin the
    lip and quick the hand,
As one who makes a last demand : "On pearls
    the dues I pay ! "

"He cannot pass ! " the watcher screamed, as to
    the chest he clung ;
"He shall not pass ! Some priceless thing he
    hideth here.   Quick — workmen bring !
  I seize this treasure for the King ! "
Old Abram stood aghast ; it seemed the knell of
    doom had rung.

III.

Red-eyed with greed and wonder,
  The crowd excited stand ;
The blows are rained like thunder
  On brazen bolt and band ;
They burst the massive hinges,
  They raise the ponderous lid,
And lo ! the peerless treasure
  That Father Abram hid :

In pearls and silk and jewels rare,
  Fit for a Pharaoh's strife ;
In flashing eyes and golden hair —
  Sat Abram's lovely wife !

THE LAST OF THE NARWHALE.

THE STORY OF AN ARCTIC NIP.

A Y, ay, I'll tell you, shipmates,
    If you care to hear the tale,
How myself and the royal yard alone
    Were left of the old Narwhale.

"A stouter ship was never launched
    Of all the Clyde-built whalers;
And forty years of a life at sea
    Haven't matched her crowd of sailors.
Picked men they were, all young and strong,
    And used to the wildest seas,
From Donegal and the Scottish coast,
    And the rugged Hebrides.
Such men as women cling to, mates,
    Like ivy round their lives:
And the day we sailed, the quays were lined
    With weeping mothers and wives.

They cried and prayed, and we gave 'em a cheer,
   In the thoughtless way of men ;
God help them, shipmates — thirty years
   They've waited and prayed since then.

"We sailed to the North, and I mind it well,
   The pity we felt, and pride
When we sighted the cliffs of Labrador
   From the sea where Hudson died.
We talked of ships that never came back,
   And when the great floes passed,
Like ghosts in the night, each moonlit peak
   Like a great war frigate's mast,
'Twas said that a ship was frozen up
   In the iceberg's awful breast,
The clear ice holding the sailor's face
   As he lay in his mortal rest.
And I've thought since then, when the ships came
         home
   That sailed for the Franklin band,
A mistake was made in the reckoning
   That looked for the crews on land.

'They're floating still,' I've said to myself,
　'And Sir John has found the goal;
The Erebus and the Terror, mates,
　Are icebergs up at the Pole!'

"We sailed due North, to Baffin's Bay,
　And cruised through weeks of light;
'Twas always day, and we slept by the bell,
　And longed for the dear old night,
And the blessed darkness left behind,
　Like a curtain round the bed;
But a month dragged on like an afternoon
　With the wheeling sun o'erhead.
We found the whales were farther still,
　The farther north we sailed;
Along the Greenland glacier coast,
　The boldest might have quailed,
Such shapes did keep us company;
　No sail in all that sea,
But thick as ships in Mersey's tide
　The bergs moved awfully

Within the current's northward stream;
  But, ere the long day's close,
We found the whales and filled the ship
  Amid the friendly floes.

"Then came a rest: the day was blown
  Like a cloud before the night;
In the South the sun went redly down—
  In the North rose another light,
Neither sun nor moon, but a shooting dawn,
  That silvered our lonely way;
It seemed we sailed in a belt of gloom,
  Upon either side, a day.
The north wind smote the sea to death;
  The pack-ice closed us round—
The Narwhale stood in the level fields
  As fast as a ship aground.
A weary time it was to wait,
  And to wish for spring to come,
With the pleasant breeze and the blessed sun,
  To open the way toward home.

"Spring came at last, the ice-fields groaned
  Like living things in pain;
They moaned and swayed, then rent amain,
  And the Narwhale sailed again.
With joy the dripping sails were loosed
  And round the vessel swung;
To cheer the crew, full south she drew,
  The shattered floes among.
We had no books in those old days
  To carry the friendly faces;
But I think the wives and lasses then
  Were held in better places.
The face of sweetheart and wife to-day
  Is locked in the sailor's chest:
But aloft on the yard, with the thought of
    home,
  The face in the heart was best.
Well, well — God knows, mates, when and
    where
  To take the things he gave;
We steered for home — but the chart was his,
  And the port ahead — the grave!

'We cleared the floes : through an open sea
  The Narwhale south'ard sailed,
Till a day came round when the white fog rose,
  And the wind astern had failed.
In front of the Greenland glacier line,
  And close to its base were we ;
Through the misty pall we could see the wall
  That beetled above the sea.
A fear like the fog crept over our hearts
  As we heard the hollow roar
Of the deep sea thrashing the cliffs of ice
  For leagues along the shore.   .

"The years have come and the years have
      gone,
  But it never wears away —
The sense I have of the sights and sounds
  That marked that woful day.
Flung here and there at the ocean's will,
  As it flung the broken floe —
What strength had we 'gainst the tiger sea
  That sports with a sailor's woe ?

The lifeless berg and the lifeful ship
   Were the same to the sullen wave,
As it swept them far from ridge to ridge,
   Till at last the Narwhale drave
With a crashing rail on the glacier wall—
   As sheer as the vessel's mast—
A crashing rail and a shivered yard;
   But the worst, we thought, was past.
The brave lads sprang to the fending work,
   And the skipper's voice rang hard:
'Aloft there, one with a ready knife—
   Cut loose that royal yard!'
I sprang to the rigging, young I was,
   And proud to be first to dare:
The yard swung free, and I turned to gaze
Toward the open sea, o'er the field of haze,
And my heart grew cold, as if frozen through,
At the moving shape that met my view—
   O Christ! what a sight was there!

"Above the fog, as I hugged the yard,
   I saw that an iceberg lay—

A berg like a mountain, closing fast —
 Not a cable's length away !
I could not see through the sheet of mist
 That covered all below,
But I heard the cheery voices still,
 And I screamed to let them know.
The cry went down, and the skipper hailed,
 But before the word could come
It died in his throat — and I knew they saw
 The shape of the closing doom !

"No sound but that — but the hail that died
 Came up through the mist to me ;
Thank God, it covered the ship like a veil,
 And I was not forced to see —
But I heard it, mates : O, I heard the rush,
 And the timbers rend and rive,
As the yard I clung to swayed and fell :
  —— I lay on the ice, alive !
Alive ! O God of mercy ! ship and crew and sea
  were gone !
The hummocked ice and the broken yard,
 And a kneeling man — alone !

" A kneeling man on a frozen hill,
　The sounds of life in the air —
All death and ice — and a minute before
　The sea and the ship were there !
I could not think they were dead and gone,
　And I listened for sound or word :
But the deep sea roar on the desolate shore
　Was the only sound I heard.
O mates, I had no heart to thank
　The Lord for the life He gave ;
I spread my arms on the ice and cried
　Aloud on my shipmates' grave.
The brave strong lads, with their strength all
　　vain,
　I called them name by name ;
And it seemed to me from the dying hearts
　A message upward came —
Ay, mates, a message, up through the ice
　From every sailor's breast :
' *Go tell our mothers and wives at home*
　To pray for us here at rest.'

" Yes, that's what it means ; 'tis a little word ;
   But, mates, the strongest ship
That ever was built is a baby's toy
   When it copes with an Arctic Nip."

DYING IN HARNESS.

ONLY a fallen horse, stretched out there on
      the road,
Stretched in the broken shafts, and crushed by
      the heavy load ;
Only a fallen horse, and a circle of wondering
      eyes
Watching the 'frighted teamster goading the beast
      to rise.

Hold ! for his toil is over — no more labor for
      him ;
See the poor neck outstretched, and the patient
      eyes grow dim ;

See on the friendly stones how peacefully rests
the head —
Thinking, if dumb beasts think, how good it is to
be dead;
After the weary journey, how restful it is to
lie
With the broken shafts and the cruel load —
waiting only to die.

Watchers, he died in harness — died in the shafts
and straps —
Fell, and the burden killed him: one of the
day's mishaps —
One of the passing wonders marking the city
road —
A toiler dying in harness, heedless of call or
goad.

Passers, crowding the pathway, staying your
steps awhile,
What is the symbol? Only death — why should
we cease to smile

At death for a beast of burden? On, through
    the busy street
That is ever and ever echoing the tread of the
    hurrying feet.

What was the sign? A symbol to touch the tire-
    less will?
Does He who taught in parables speak in par-
    ables still?
The seed on the rock is wasted — on heedless
    hearts of men,
That gather and sow and grasp and lose — labor
    and sleep — and then —
Then for the prize!——A crowd in the street
    of ever-echoing tread —
The toiler, crushed by the heavy load, is there in
    his harness — dead !

GOLU.

ONCE I had a little sweetheart
   In the land of the Malay, —
Such a little yellow sweetheart!
   Warm and peerless as the day
Of her own dear sunny island,
   Keimah, in the far, far East,
Where the mango and banana
   Made us many a merry feast.

Such a little copper sweetheart
   Was my Golu, plump and round,
With her hair all blue-black streaming
   O'er her to the very ground.
Soft and clear as dew-drop clinging
   To a grass blade was her eye ;
For the heart below was purer
   Than the hill-stream whispering by.

Costly robes were not for Golu:
　　No more raiment did she need
Than the milky budding breadfruit,
　　Or the lily of the mead;
And she was my little sweetheart
　　Many a sunny summer day,
When we ate the fragrant guavas,
　　In the land of the Malay.

Life was laughing then.　Ah! **Golu,**
　　Do you think of that old time,
And of all the tales I told you
　　Of my colder Western clime?
Do you think how happy were **we**
　　When we sailed to strip the **palm,**
And we made a latteen arbor
　　Of the boat-sail in the calm?

They may call you semi-**savage,**
　　Golu!　I cannot forget
How I poised my little sweet**heart**
　　Like a copper statuette.

Now my path lies through the cities;
But they cannot drive away
My sweet dreams of little Golu
And the land of the Malay.

UNDER THE RIVER

CLEAR and bright, from the snowy height,
  The joyous stream to the plain descended:
Rich sands of gold were washed and rolled
  To the turbid marsh where its pure life ended.

From stainless snow to the moor below
  The heart like the brook · has a waning mis-
    sion:
The buried dream in life's sluggish stream
  Is the golden sand of our young ambition.

HIDDEN SINS.

FOR every sin that comes before the light,
　　And leaves an outward blemish on the soul,
How many, darker, cower out of sight, -
　　And burrow, blind and silent, like the mole.
And like the mole, too, with its busy feet
　　That dig and dig a never-ending cave,
Our hidden sins gnaw through the soul, and **meet**
　　And feast upon each other in its grave.

A buried sin is like a covered sore
　　That spreads and festers 'neath a painted face;
And no man's art can heal it evermore,
　　But only His — the Surgeon's — promised **grace.**
Who hides a sin is like the hunter who
　　Once warmed a frozen adder with his breath,
And when he placed it near his heart it flew
　　With poisoned fangs and stung that heart to death.

A sculptor once a granite statue made,
　　One-sided only, just to fit its place:
The unseen side was monstrous; so men shade
　　Their evil acts behind a smiling face.
O blind! O foolish! thus our sins to hide,
　　And force our pleading hearts the gall to sip;
O cowards! who must eat the myrrh, that Pride
　　May smile like Virtue with a lying lip.

A sin admitted is nigh half atoned;
　　And while the fault is red and freshly done,
If we but drop our eyes and think, — 'tis owned, —
　　'Tis half forgiven, half the crown is won.
But if we heedless let it reck and rot,
　　Then pile a mountain on its grave, and turn,
With smiles to all the world, — that tainted spot
　　Beneath the mound will never cease to burn.

UNSPOKEN WORDS.

THE kindly words that rise within the heart,
　　And thrill it with their sympathetic tone,
But die ere spoken, fail to play their part,
　　And claim a merit that is not their own.
The kindly word unspoken is a sin, —
　　A sin that wraps itself in purest guise,
And tells the heart that, doubting, looks within,
　　That not in speech, but thought, the virtue lies.

But 'tis not so: another heart may thirst
　　For that kind word, as Hagar in the wild —
Poor banished Hagar! — prayed a well might burst
　　From out the sand to save her parching child.
And loving eyes that cannot see the mind
　　Will watch the expected movement of the lip:
Ah! can ye let its cutting silence wind
　　Around that heart, and scathe it like a whip?

Unspoken words, like treasures in the mine,
  Are valueless until we give them birth:
Like unfound gold their hidden beauties shine,
  Which God has made to bless and gild the earth.
How sad 'twould be to see a master's hand
  Strike glorious notes upon a voiceless lute!
But oh! what pain when, at God's own command,
  A heart-string thrills with kindness, but is mute!

Then hide it not, the music of the soul,
  Dear sympathy, expressed with kindly voice,
But let it like a shining river roll
  To deserts dry, — to hearts that would rejoice.
Oh! let the symphony of kindly words
  Sound for the poor, the friendless, and the weak;
And He will bless you, — He who struck these
    chords
  Will strike another when in turn you seek.

THE POISON-FLOWER.

IN the evergreen shade of an Austral wood,
  Where the long branches laced above,
    Through which all day it seemed
    The sweet sunbeams down-gleamed
  Like the rays of a young mother's love,
When she hides her glad face with her hands and
      peeps
  At the youngling that crows on her knee:
    'Neath such ray-shivered shade,
    In a banksia glade,
  Was this flower first shown to me.

A rich pansy it was, with a small white lip
  And a wonderful purple hood;
    And your eye caught the sheen
    Of its leaves, parrot-green,
  Down the dim gothic aisles of the wood.
And its foliage rich on the moistureless sand

Made you long for its odorous breath ;
    But ah ! 'twas to take
    To your bosom a snake,
For its pestilent fragrance was death.

And I saw it again, in a far northern land, —
    Not a pansy, not purple and white ;
      Yet in beauteous guise
      Did this poison-plant rise,
    Fair and fatal again to my sight.
And men longed for her kiss and her odorous breath
    When no friend was beside them to tell
      That to kiss was to die,
      That her truth was a lie,
    And her beauty a soul-killing spell.

MY MOTHER'S MEMORY.

THERE is one bright star in heaven
    Ever shining in my night;
God to me one guide has given,
    Like the sailor's beacon-light,
Set on every shoal and danger,
    Sending out its warning ray
To the home-bound weary stranger
    Looking for the land-locked bay.

In my farthest, wildest wanderings
    I have turned me to that love,
As a diver, 'neath the water,
    Turns to watch the light above.

THE OLD SCHOOL CLOCK.

OLD memories rush o'er my mind just now
   Of faces and friends of the past;
Of that happy time when life's dream was all bright.
   Ere the clear sky of youth was o'ercast.
Very dear are those mem'ries, — they 've clung
    round my heart,
   And bravely withstood Time's rude shock;
But not one is more hallowed or dear to me now
   Than the face of the old school clock.

'Twas a quaint old clock with a quaint old face,
   And great iron weights and chain;
It stopped when it liked, and before it struck
   It creaked as if 'twere in pain.

It had seen many years, and it seemed to say,
   " I 'm one of the real old stock,"
To the youthful fry, who with reverence looked
   On the face of the old school clock.

How many a time have I labored to sketch
   That yellow and time-honored face,
With its basket of flowers, its figures and hands,
   And the weights and the chains in their place !
How oft have I gazed with admiring eye,
   As I sat on the wooden block,
And pondered and guessed at the wonderful things
   That were inside that old school clock !

What a terrible frown did the old clock wear
   To the truant, who timidly cast
An anxious eye on those merciless hands,
   That for him had been moving too fast !
But its frown soon changed ; for it loved to smile
   On the thoughtless, noisy flock,
And it creaked and whirred and struck with glee, --
   Did that genial, good-humored old clock.

Well, years had passed, and my mind was filled
  With the world, its cares and ways,
When again I stood in that little school
  Where I passed my boyhood's days.
My old friend was gone! and there hung a thing
  That my sorrow seemed to mock,
As I gazed with a tear and a softened heart
  At a new-fashioned Yankee clock.

'Twas a gaudy thing with bright painted sides,
  And it looked with insolent stare
On the desks and the seats and on every thing old
  And I thought of the friendly air
Of the face that I missed, with its weights and
      chains, —
  All gone to the auctioneer's block:
'Tis a thing of the past, — never more shall I see
  But in memory that old school clock.

'Tis the way of the world: old friends pass away,
  And fresh faces arise in their stead;
But still 'mid the din and the bustle of life
  We cherish fond thoughts of the dead.

Yes, dearly those memories cling round my
    heart,
And bravely withstand Time's rude shock;
But not one is more dear or more hallowed to me
    Than the face of that old school clock.

MARY.

DEAR honored name, beloved for human ties,
    But loved and honored first that One was
    given
In living proof to erring mortal eyes
    That our poor earth is near akin to heaven.

Sweet word of dual meaning: one of grace,
    And born of our kind advocate above; ·
And one by memory linked to that dear face
    That blessed my childhood with its mother-
    love,

And taught me first the simple prayer, "To thee,
Poor banished sons of Eve, we send our cries."
Through mist of years, those words recall to me
A childish face upturned to loving eyes.

And yet to some the name of Mary bears
No special meaning and no gracious power;
In that dear word they seek for hidden snares,
As wasps find poison in the sweetest flower.

But faithful hearts can see, o'er doubts and fears,
The Virgin link that binds the Lord to earth;
Which to the upturned trusting face appears
A more than angel, though of human birth.

The sweet-faced moon reflects on cheerless night
The rays of hidden sun to rise to-morrow;
So unseen God still lets His promised light,
Through holy Mary, shine upon our sorrow.

A LEGEND OF THE BLESSED VIRGIN.

THE day of Joseph's marriage unto Mary,
    In thoughtful mood he said unto his wife,
" Behold, I go into a far-off country
    To labor for thee, and to make thy life
And home all sweet and peaceful." And the Virgin
    Unquestioning beheld her spouse depart :
Then lived she many days of musing gladness,
    Not knowing that God's hand was round her
      heart.

And dreaming thus one day within her chamber,
    She wept with speechless bliss, when lo ! the face
Of white-winged angel Gabriel rose before her,
    And bowing spoke, " Hail ! Mary, full of grace,

The Lord is with thee, and among the nations
    Forever blessed is thy chosen name."
The angel vanished, and the Lord's high Presence
    With untold glory to the Virgin came.

A season passed of joy unknown to mortals,
    When Joseph came with what his toil had won,
And broke the brooding ecstasy of Mary,
    Whose soul was ever with her promised Son.
But nature's jealous fears encircled Joseph,
    And round his heart in darkening doubts held
      sway.
He looked upon his spouse cold-eyed, and pondered
    How he could put her from his sight away.

And once, when moody thus within his garden,
    The gentle girl besought for some ripe fruit
That hung beyond her reach, the old man an-
    swered,
    With face averted, harshly to her suit:
" I will not serve thee, woman! Thou hast wronged
    me :

I heed no more thy words and actions mild ;
If fruit thou wantest, thou canst henceforth ask it
   From him, the father of thy unborn child ! ''

But ere the words had root within her hearing,
   The Virgin's face was glorified anew ;
And Joseph, turning, sank within her presence,
   And knew indeed his wondrous dreams were
      true.
For there before the sandalled feet of Mary
   The kingly tree had bowed its top, and she
Had pulled and eaten from its prostrate branches,
   As if unconscious of the mystery.

THE LOSS OF THE EMIGRANTS. *

FOR months and years, with penury and want
  And heart-sore envy did they dare to cope;
And mite by mite was saved from earnings scant,
  To buy, some future day, the God-sent hope.

They trod the crowded streets of hoary towns,
  Or tilled from year to year the wearied fields,
And in the shadow of the golden crowns
  They gasped for sunshine and the health it yields.

They turned from homes all cheerless, child and
    man,
  With kindly feelings only for the soil,
And for the kindred faces, pinched and wan,
  That prayed, and stayed, unwilling, at their toil.

They lifted up their faces to the Lord,
  And read His answer in the westering sun
That called them ever as a shining word,
  And beckoned seaward as the rivers run.

* The steamer Atlantic was wrecked near Halifax, N.S., April 1st, 1873,
and 560 lives lost.

They looked their last, wet-eyed, on Swedish
    hills,
  On German villages and English dales;
Like brooks that grow from many mountain rills
    The peasant-stream flowed out from Irish vales.

Their grief at parting was not all a grief,
    But blended sweetly with the joy to come,
When from full store they spared the rich relief
    To gladden all the dear ones left at home.

"We thank thee, God!" they cried; "the cruel
    gate
  That barred our lives has swung beneath Thy
    hand;
Behind our ship now frowns the cruel fate,
    Before her smiles the teeming Promised Land!"

Alas! when shown in mercy or in wrath,
    How weak we are to read God's awful lore!
His breath protected on the stormy path,
    And dashed them lifeless on the promised
    shore!

His hand sustained them in the parting woe,
　　And gave bright vision to the heart of each
His waters bore them where they wished to go,
　　Then swept them seaward from the very beach !

Their home is reached, their fetters now are riven,
　　Their humble toil is o'er, — their rest has come ;
A land was promised and a land is given, —
　　But, oh ! God help the waiting ones at home !

WITHERED SNOWDROPS.

THEY came in the early spring-days,
　　With the first refreshing showers
And I watched the growing beauty
　　Of the little drooping flowers.

They had no bright hues to charm **me**,
　　No gay painting to allure;
But they made me think of angels,
　　They were all so white and pure.

In the early morns I saw them,
　　Dew-drops clinging to each bell,
And the first glad sunbeam hasting
　　Just to kiss them ere they fell.

Daily grew their spotless beauty;
　　But I feared when chill winds blew

They were all too frail and tender, —
 And alas! my fears were true.

One glad morn I went to see them
 While the bright drops gemmed their snow
And one angel flower was withered,
 Its fair petals drooping low.

Its white sister's tears fell on it,
 And the sunbeam sadly shone;
For its innocence was withered,
 And its purity was gone.

Still I left it there: I could not
 Tear it rudely from its place;
It might rise again, and summer
 Might restore its vanished grace.

But my hopes grew weaker, weaker,
 And my heart with grief was pained
When I knew it must be severed
 From the innocence it stained.

I must take it from the pure ones:
  Henceforth they must live apart.
But I could not cut my flow'ret —
  My lost angel — from my heart.

Oft I think of that dead snowdrop,
  Think with sorrow, when I meet,
Day by day, the poor lost flowers, —
  Sullied snowdrops of the street.

They were pure once, loved and loving,
  And there still lives good within.
Ah! speak gently to them: harsh words
  Will not lead them from their sin.

The are not like withered flowers
  That can never bloom again:
They can rise, bright angel snowdrops,
  Purified from every stain.

THE WAIL OF TWO CITIES.

CHICAGO, OCTOBER 9, 1871.

GAUNT in the midst of the prairie,
　　She who was once so fair;
Charred and rent are her garments,
Heavy and dark like cerements;
　　Silent, but round her the air
Plaintively wails, "Miserere!"

Proud like a beautiful maiden,
　　Art-like from forehead to feet,
Was she till pressed like a leman
Close to the breast of the demon,
　　Lusting for one so sweet,
So were her shoulders laden.

Friends she had, rich in her treasures :
　　Shall the old taunt be true, —
Fallen, they turn their cold faces,
Seeking new wealth-gilded places,
　　Saying we never knew
Aught of her smiles or her pleasures ?

Silent she stands on the prairie,
　　Wrapped in her fire-scathed sheet :
Around her, thank God ! is the **Nation,**
Weeping for her desolation,
　　Pouring its gold at her feet,
Answering her "Miserere !"

BOSTON, NOVEMBER 9, 1872.

O broad-breasted Queen among Nations !
　　O Mother, so strong in thy youth !
Has the Lord looked upon thee in ire,
And willed thou be chastened by fire,
　　Without any ruth ?

Has the Merciful tired of His mercy,
        And turned from thy sinning in wrath,
That the world with raised hands sees and pities
Thy desolate daughters, thy cities,
        Despoiled on their path?

One year since thy youngest was stricken:
        Thy eldest lies stricken to-day.
Ah! God, was thy wrath without pity,
To tear the strong heart from our city,
        And cast it away?

O Father! forgive us our doubting;
        The stain from our weak souls efface;
Thou rebukest, we know, but to chasten;
Thy hand has but fallen to hasten
        Return to thy grace.

Let us rise purified from our ashes
        As sinners have risen who grieved;
Let us show that twice-sent desolation
On every true heart in the nation
        Has conquest achieved.

THE FISHERMEN OF WEXFORD.

THERE is an old tradition sacred held in Wex-
 ford town,
That says: " Upon St. Martin's eve no net shall be
 let down;
No fishermen of Wexford shall, upon that holy day,
Set sail or cast a line within the scope of Wexford
 Bay."
The tongue that framed the order, or the time, no
 one could tell;
And no one ever questioned, but the people kept it
 well.
And never in man's memory was fisher known to
 leave
The little town of Wexford on the good St. Martin's
 Eve.

Alas! alas for Wexford! once upon that holy
    day
Came a wondrous shoal of herring to the waters of
    the Bay.
The fishers and their families stood out upon the
    beach,
And all day watched with wistful eyes the wealth
    they might not reach.
Such shoal was never seen before, and keen regrets
    went round'—
Alas! alas for Wexford! Hark! what is that
    grating sound?
The boats' keels on the shingle! Mothers! wives!
    ye well may grieve, —
The fishermen of Wexford mean to sail on Martin's
    Eve!

"Oh, stay ye!" cried the women wild. "Stay!"
    cried the men white-haired;
"And dare ye not to do this thing your fathers
    never dared.

No man can thrive who tempts the Lord!"
    "Away!" they cried: "the Lord
Ne'er sent a shoal of fish but as a fisherman's re-
    ward."
And scoffingly they said, "To-night our nets shall
    sweep the Bay,
And take the Saint who guards it, should he come
    across our way!"
The keels have touched the water, and the crews
    are in each boat;
And on St. Martin's Eve the Wexford fishers are
    afloat!

The moon is shining coldly on the sea and on the
    land,
On dark faces in the fishing-fleet and pale ones on
    the strand,
As seaward go the daring boats, and heavenward
    the cries
Of kneeling wives and mothers with uplifted hands
    and eyes.

"O Holy Virgin! be their guard!" the weeping
    women cried;
The old men, sad and silent, watched the boats
    cleave through the tide,
As past the farthest headland, past the lighthouse,
    in a line
The fishing-fleet went seaward through the phos-
    phor-lighted brine.

Oh, pray, ye wives and mothers! All your prayers
    they sorely need
To save them from the wrath they've roused by
    their rebellious greed.
Oh! white-haired men and little babes, and weep-
    ing sweethearts, pray
To God to spare the fishermen to-night in Wexford
    Bay!

The boats have reached good offing, and, as out the
    nets are thrown,
The hearts ashore are chilled to hear the soughing
    sea wind's moan:

Like to a human heart that loved, and hoped for
  some return,
To find at last but hatred, so the sea-wind seemed
  to mourn.
But ah! the Wexford fishermen! their nets did
  scarcely sink
One inch below the foam, when, lo! the daring
  boatmen shrink
With sudden awe and whitened lips and glaring
  eyes agape,
For breast-high, threatening, from the sea uprose a
  Human Shape!

Beyond them, — in the moonlight, — hand upraised
  and awful mien,
Waving back and pointing landwards, breast-high
  in the sea 'twas seen.
Thrice it waved and thrice it pointed, — then, with
  clenchéd hand upraised,
The awful shape went down before the fishers as
  they gazed!

Gleaming whitely through the water, fathoms deep
    they saw its frown, —

They saw its white hand clenched above it, — sink-
    ing slowly down !

And then there was a rushing 'neath the boats, and
    every soul

Was thrilled with greed: they knew it was the
    seaward-going shoal !

Defying the dread warning, every face was sternly
    set,

And wildly did they ply the oar, and wildly haul
    the net.

But two boats' crews obeyed the sign, — God-fearing
    men were they, —

They cut their lines and left their nets, and home-
    ward sped away ;

But darkly rising sternwards did God's wrath in
    tempest sweep,

And they, of all the fishermen, that night escaped
    the deep.

Oh, wives and mothers, sweethearts, sires! well
    might ye mourn next day:
For seventy fishers' corpses strewed the shores of
    Wexford Bay!

THE FEAST OF THE GAEL.

ST. PATRICK'S DAY.

I.

WHAT a union of hearts is the love of a mother
  When races of men in her name unite !
For love of Old Erin, and love of each other,
  The boards of the Gael are full to-night !
Their millions of men have one toast and one
    topic —
  Their feuds laid aside and their envies re-
    moved ;
From the pines of the Pole to the palms of the
    Tropic,
  They drink : "The dear Land we have prayed
    for and loved !"
They are One by the bond of a time-honored
    fashion ;
  Though strangers may see but the lights of
    their feast,

Beneath lies the symbol of faith and of passion
   Alike of the Pagan and Christian priest!

II.

When native laws by native kings
   At Tara were decreed,
The grand old Gheber worship
   Was the form of Erin's creed.
The Sun, Life-Giver, was God on high;
   Men worshipped the Power they saw;
And they kept the faith as the ages rolled
   By the solemn Beltane law.
Each year, on the Holy Day, was quenched
   The household fires of the land;
And the Druid priest, at the midnight hour,
   Brought forth the flaming brand,—
The living spark for the Nation's hearths,—
   From the Monarch's hand it came,
Whose fire at Tara spread the sign —
   And the people were One by the flame!

And Baal was God! till Patrick came,
　　By the Holy Name inspired;
On the Beltane night, in great Tara's sight,
　　His pile at Slane was fired.
And the deed that was death was the Nation's life,
　　And the doom of the Pagan bane;
For Erin still keeps Beltane night,
　　But lights her lamp at Slane!

Though fourteen centuries pile their dust
　　On the mound of the Druid's grave,
TO-NIGHT IS THE BELTANE! Bright the fire
　　That Holy Patrick gave!
TO-NIGHT IS THE BELTANE! Let him heed
　　Who studieth creed and race:
Old times and gods are dead, and we
　　Are far from the ancient place;
The waves of centuries, war, and waste,
　　Of famine, gallows, and gaol,
Have swept our land; but the world to-night
　　Sees the Beltane Fire of the Gael!

III.

O land of sad fate! like a desolate queen,
  Who remembers in sorrow the crown of her
    glory,
The love of thy children not strangely is seen —
  For humanity weeps at thy heart-touching
    story.
Strong heart in affliction! that draweth thy foes
  'Till they love thee more dear than thine own
    generation :
Thy strength is increased as thy life-current
    flows,—
  What were death to another is Ireland's salva-
    tion !
God scatters her sons like the seed on the lea,
  And they root where they fall, be it mountain
    or furrow ;
They come to remain and remember ; and she
  In their growth will rejoice in a blissful to-
    morrow !

They sing in strange lands the sweet songs of
    their home,
  Their emerald Zion enthroned in the billows;
To work, not to weep by the rivers they come:
  Their harps are not hanged in despair on the
    willows.
The hope of the mother beats youthful and
    strong,
  Responsive and true to her children's pulsa-
    tions,
No petrified heart has she saved from the
    wrong —
  Our Niobe lives for her place 'mong the
    nations!

Then drink, all her sons — be they Keltic or
    Danish,
  Or Norman or Saxon — one mantle was o'er us;
Let race lines, and creed lines, and every line,
    vanish —
  We drink as the Gael: "To the Mother that
    bore us!"

AT FREDERICKSBURG.—DEC. 13, 1862.

GOD send us peace, and keep red strife away;
    But should it come, God send us men and
    steel!
The land is dead that dare not face the day
    When foreign danger threats the common weal.

Defenders strong are they that homes defend;
    From ready arms the spoiler keeps afar.
Well blest the country that has sons to lend
    From trades of peace to learn the trade of war.

Thrice blest the nation that has every son
    A soldier, ready for the warning sound;
Who marches homeward when the fight is done,
    To swing the hammer and to till the ground.

Call back that morning, with its lurid light,
    When through our land the awful war-bell tolled;

When lips were mute, and women's faces white
   As the pale cloud that out from Sumter rolled.

Call back that morn: an instant all were dumb,
   As if the shot had struck the Nation's life;
Then cleared the smoke, and rolled the calling
    drum,
   And men streamed in to meet the coming
    strife.

They closed the ledger and they stilled the loom,
   The plough left rusting in the prairie farm;
They saw but "Union" in the gathering gloom;
   The tearless women helped the men to arm;

Brigades from towns — each village sent its band:
   German and Irish — every race and faith;
There was no question then of native land,
   But — love the Flag and follow it to death.

No need to tell their tale: through every age
   The splendid story shall be sung and said;

But let me draw one picture from the page —
  For words of song embalm the hero dead.

———

The smooth hill is bare, and the cannons are
    planted,
  Like Gorgon fates shading its terrible brow;
The word has been passed that the stormers are
    wanted,
  And Burnside's battalions are mustering now.
The armies stand by to behold the dread meet-
    ing;
  The work must be done by a desperate few;
The black-mouthéd guns on the height give them
    greeting —
  From gun-mouth to plain every grass blade in
    view.
Strong earthworks are there, and the rifles be-
    hind them
  Are Georgia militia — an Irish brigade —
Their caps have green badges, as if to remind
    them
  Of all the brave record their country has made.

The stormers go forward — the Federals cheer
    them ;
  They breast the smooth hillside — the black
    mouths are dumb ;
The riflemen lie in the works till they near them,
  And cover the stormers as upward they come.
Was ever a death-march so grand and so solemn?
  At last, the dark summit with flame is enlined ;
The great guns belch doom on the sacrificed
    column,
  That reels from the height, leaving hundreds
    behind.
The armies are hushed — there is no cause for
    cheering :
  The fall of brave men to brave men is a pain.
Again come the stormers ! and as they are nearing
  The flame-sheeted rifle-lines, reel back again.
And so till full noon come the Federal masses —
  Flung back from the height, as the cliff flings a
    wave ;
Brigade on brigade to the death-struggle passes,
  No wavering rank till it steps on the grave.

Then comes a brief lull, and the smoke-pall is
 lifted,
The green of the hillside no longer is seen;
The dead soldiers lie as the sea-weed is drifted,
 The earthworks still held by the badges of
 green.
Have they quailed? is the word. No: again
 they are forming —
Again comes a column to death and defeat!
What is it in these who shall now do the storming
 That makes every Georgian spring to his feet?

"O God! what a pity!" they cry in their cover,
 As rifles are readied and bayonets made tight;
"'Tis Meagher and his fellows! their caps have
 green clover;
 'Tis Greek to Greek now for the rest of the
 fight!"
Twelve hundred the column, their rent flag before
 them,   •
 With Meagher at their head, they have dashed
 at the hill!

Their foemen are proud of the country that bore
    them ;
  But, Irish in love, they are enemies still.
Out rings the fierce word, "Let them have it!"
    the rifles
  Are emptied point-blank in the hearts of the
    foe :
It is green against green, but a principle stifles
  The Irishman's love in the Georgian's blow.
The column has reeled, but it is not defeated ;
  In front of the guns they re-form and attack ;
Six times they have done it, and six times re-
    treated ;
  Twelve hundred they came, and two hundred
    go back.
Two hundred go back with the chivalrous story ;
  The wild day is closed in the night's solemn
    shroud ;
A thousand lie dead, but their death was a
    glory
  That calls not for tears — the Green Badges
    are proud !

Bright honor be theirs who for honor were fear-
    less,
  Who charged for their flag to the grim cannon's
    mouth;
And honor to them who were true, though not
    tearless,—
  Who bravely that day kept the cause of the
    South.
The quarrel is done — God avert such another;
  The lesson it brought we should evermore
    heed:
Who loveth the Flag is a man and a brother,
  No matter what birth or what race or what
    creed.

THE PRIESTS OF IRELAND.

["The time has arrived when the interests of our country require from us, as priests and as Irishmen, a public pronouncement on the vital question of Home Rule. . . . We suggest the holding of an aggregate meeting in Dublin, of the representatives of all interested in this great question — and they are the entire people, without distinction of creed or class — for the purpose of placing, by constitutional means, on a broad and definite basis, the nation's demand for the restoration of its plundered rights." — *Extract from the Declaration of the Bishop and Priests of the Diocese of Cloyne, made on Sept. 15, 1873.*]

YOU have waited, Priests of Ireland, until the
    hour was late:
You have stood with folded arms until 'twas
    asked — Why do they wait?
By the fever and the famine you have seen your
    flocks grow thin,
Till the whisper hissed through Ireland that your
    silence was a sin.
You have looked with tearless eyes on fleets of
    exile-laden ships,
And the hands that stretched toward Ireland
    brought no tremor to your lips;

In the sacred cause of freedom you have seen
    your people band,
And they looked to you for sympathy : you never
    stirred a hand ;
But you stood upon the altar, with their blood
    within your veins,
And you bade the pale-faced people to be patient
    in their chains !
Ah, you told them — it was cruel — but you said
    they were not true
To the holy faith of Patrick, if they were not
    ruled by you ;
Yes, you told them from the altar — they, the
    vanguard of the Faith —
With your eyes like flint against them — that
    their banding was a death —
Was a death to something holy : till the heart-
    wrung people cried
That their priests had turned against them — that
    they had no more a guide —
That the English gold had bought you — yes,
    they said it — but they lied !

Yea, they lied, they sinned, not knowing you —
    they had not gauged your love :
Heaven bless you, Priests of Ireland, for the wis-
    dom from above,
For the strength that made you, loving them,
    crush back the tears that rose
When your country's heart was quiv'ring 'neath
    the statesman's muffled blows :
You saw clearer far than they did, and you
    grieved for Ireland's pain ;
But you did not rouse the people — and your
    silence was their gain ;
For too often has the peasant dared to dash his
    naked arm
'Gainst the sabre of the soldier : but you shielded
    him from harm,
And your face was set against him — though your
    heart was with his hand
When it flung aside the plough to snatch a pike
    for fatherland !

O, God bless you, Priests of Ireland! You
    were waiting with a will,
You were waiting with a purpose when you bade
    your flocks be still;
And you preached from off your altars not alone
    the Word Sublime,
But your silence preached to Irishmen — "Be
    patient: bide your time!"
And they heard you, and obeyed, as well as out-
    raged men could do : —
Only some, who loved poor Ireland, but who
    erred in doubting you,
Doubting you, who could not tell them why you
    spake the strange behest —
You, who saw the day was coming when the
    moral strength was best —
You, whose hearts were sore with looking on your
    country's quick decay —
You, whose chapel seats were empty and your
    people fled away —
You, who marked amid the fields where once the
    peasant's cabin stood —

You, who saw your kith and kindred swell the
    emigration flood —

You, the *soggarth* in the famine, and the helper
    in the frost —

You, whose shadow was a sunshine when all
    other hope was lost —

Yes, they doubted — and you knew it — but you
    never said a word;

Only preached, "Be still: be patient!" and,
    thank God, your voice was heard.

Now, the day foreseen is breaking — it has
    dawned upon the land,

And the priests still preach in Ireland: do they
    bid their flocks disband?

Do they tell them still to suffer and be silent?
    No! their words

Flash from Dublin Bay to Connaught, brighter
    than the gleam of swords!

Flash from Donegal to Kerry, and from Water-
    ford to Clare,

And the nationhood awaking thrills the sorrow-
    laden air.

Well they judged their time—they waited till the
    bar was glowing white,
Then they swung it on the anvil, striking down
    with earnest might,
And the burning sparks that scatter lose no
    lustre on their way,
Till five million hearts in Ireland and ten millions
    far away
Feel the first good blow, and answer; and they
    will not rest with one:
Now the first is struck, the anvil shows the labor
    well begun;
Swing them in with lusty sinew and the work will
    soon be done!
Let them sound from hoary Cashel; Kerry,
    Meath, and Ross stand forth;
Let them ring from Cloyne and Tuam and the
    Primate of the North;
Ask not class or creed: let "Ireland!" be the
    talismanic word;
Let the blessed sound of unity from North to
    South be heard;

Carve the words: "No creed distinctions!" on
    O'Connell's granite tomb,
And his dust will feel their meaning and rekindle
    in the gloom.
Priest to priest, to sound the summons — and the
    answer, man to man;
With the people round the standard, and the
    prelates in the van.
Let the heart of Ireland's hoping keep this golden
    rule of Cloyne
Till the Orange fades from Derry and the shadow
    from the Boyne.
Let the words be carried outward till the farthest
    lands they reach:
"After Christ, their country's freedom do the
    Irish prelates preach!"

RELEASED — JANUARY, 1878.*

THEY are free at last! They can face the
    sun;
  Their hearts now throb with the world's
    pulsation;
Their prisons are open — their night is done;
  'Tis England's mercy and reparation!

The years of their doom have slowly sped —
  Their limbs are withered — their ties are riven;
Their children are scattered, their friends are
    dead —
  But the prisons are open — the "crime" for-
    given.

* On the 5th of January, 1878, three of the Irish political prisoners, who had been confined since 1866, were set at liberty. The released men were received by their fellow-countrymen in London. "They are well," said the report, "but they look prematurely old."

God! what a threshold they stand upon :
  The world has passed on while they were
      buried ;
In the glare of the sun they walk alone
  On the grass-grown track where the crowd has
   • hurried.

Haggard and broken and seared with pain,
  They seek the remembered friends and places :
Men shuddering turn, and gaze again
  At the deep-drawn lines on their altered faces.

What do they read on the pallid page ?
  What is the tale of these woful letters ?
A lesson as old as their country's age,
  Of a love that is stronger than stripes and
      fetters.

In the blood of the slain some dip their blade,
  And swear by the stain the foe to follow :
But a deadlier oath might here be made,
  On the wasted bodies and faces hollow.

Irishmen! You who have kept the peace —
　Look on these forms diseased and broken:
Believe, if you can, that their late release,
　When their lives are sapped, is a good-will
　　token.

Their hearts are the bait on England's hook;
　For this are they dragged from her hopeless
　　prison;
She reads her doom in the Nations' book —
　She fears the day that has darkly risen;

She reaches her hand for Ireland's aid —
　Ireland, scourged, contemned, derided;
She begs from the beggar her hate has made;
　She seeks for the strength her guile divided.

She offers a bribe — ah, God above!
　Behold the price of the desecration:
The hearts she has tortured for Irish love
　She brings as a bribe to the Irish nation!

O, blind and cruel !   She fills her cup
   With   conquest   and   pride,   till   its   red   wine
      splashes :
But shrieks at the draught as she drinks it up —
   Her wine has been turned to blood and ashes.

We know her—our Sister !   Come on the storm !
   God send it soon and sudden upon her :
The race she has shattered and sought to deform
   Shall laugh as she drinks the black dishonor.

THE PATRIOT'S GRAVE.

READ AT THE EMMET CENTENNIAL IN BOSTON, MARCH 4, 1878.

["I am going to my cold and silent grave — my lamp of life is nearly extinguished. I have parted with everything that was dear to me in this life for my country's cause — with the idol of my soul, the object of my affections: my race is run, the grave opens to receive me, and I sink into its bosom! I have but one request to make at my departure from this world — it is the charity of its silence! Let no man write my epitaph; for, as no man who knows my motives dare now vindicate them, let not ignorance nor prejudice asperse them. Let them rest in obscurity and peace! Let my memory be left in oblivion, and my tomb uninscribed, until other times and other men can do justice to my character. When my country takes her place among the nations of the earth, then, and not till then, let my epitaph be written." — *Speech of Robert Emmet in the Dock.*]

I.

TEAR down the crape from the column ! Let
    the shaft stand white and fair !
Be silent the wailing music — there is no death
    in the air !
We come not in plaint or sorrow — no tears may
    dim our sight :
We dare not weep o'er the epitaph we have not
    dared to write.

Come hither with glowing faces, the sire, the
    youth, and the child ;
This grave is a shrine for reverent hearts and
    hands that are undefiled :
Its ashes are inspiration ; it giveth us strength to
    bear,
And sweepeth away dissension, and nerveth the
    will to dare.

In the midst of the tombs, a Gravestone — and
    written thereon no word !
And behold, at the head of the grave, a gibbet, a
    torch, and a sword !
And the people kneel by the gibbet, and pray by
    the nameless stone
For the torch to be lit, and the name to be writ,
    and the sword's red work to be done !

II.

With pride and not with grief
We lay this century leaf
Upon the tomb, with hearts that do not falter :

A few brief, toiling years
Since fell the nation's tears,
And lo, the patriot's gibbet is an altar !

The people that are blest
Have him they love the best
To mount the martyr's scaffold when they need
      him ;
And vain the cords that bind
While the nation's steadfast mind,
Like the needle to the pole, is true to freedom !

III.

Three powers there are that dominate the
    world —
   Fraud, Force, and Right—and two oppress the
    one :
The bolts of Fraud and Force like twins are
    hurled —
   Against them ever standeth Right alone.

Cyclopian strokes the brutal allies give :
    Their fetters massive and their dungeon walls ;
Beneath their yoke, weak nations cease to live,
    And valiant Right itself defenceless falls !

Defaced is law, and justice slain at birth ;
    Good men are broken — malefactors thrive ;
But, when the tyrants tower o'er the earth,
    Behind their wheels strong right is still alive !

Alive, like seed that God's own hand has sown —
    Like seed that lieth in the lowly furrow,
But springs to life when wintry winds are blown :
    To-day the earth is gray — 'tis green to-
        morrow.

The roots strike deep despite the rulers' power,
    The plant grows strong with summer sun and
        rain,
Till Autumn bursts the deep red-hearted flower,
    And freedom marches to the front again !

While slept the right, and reigned the dual
    wrong,
Unchanged, unchecked, for half a thousand
    years,
In tears of blood we cried, "O Lord, how long?"
And even God seemed deaf to Erin's tears.

But when she lay all weak and bruised and
    broken,
    Her white limbs seared with cruel chain and
        thorn — '
As bursts the cloud, the lightning word was
    spoken,
    God's seed took root — His crop of men was
        born!

With one deep breath began the land's progres-
    sion:
On every field the seeds of freedom fell:
Burke, Grattan, Flood, and Curran in the ses-
    sion —
    Fitzgerald, Sheares, and Emmet in the cell!

Such teachers soon aroused the dormant nation —
  Such sacrifice insured the endless fight:
The voice of Grattan smote wrong's domina-
  tion —
    The death of Emmet sealed the cause of
    right!

IV.

Richest of gifts to a nation! Death with the
  living crown!
Type of ideal manhood to the people's heart
  brought down!

Fount of the hopes we cherish — Test of the
  things we do;
Gorgon's face for the traitor — Talisman for the
  true!

Sweet is the love of a woman, and sweet is the
  kiss of a child;
Sweet is the tender strength, and the bravery of
  the mild;

But sweeter than all, for embracing all, is the
    young life's peerless price —
The young heart laid on the altar, as a nation's
    sacrifice.

How can the debt be cancelled? Prayers and
    tears we may give —
But how recall the anguish of hearts that have
    ceased to live?

Flushed with the pride of genius — filled with the
    strength of life --
Thrilled with delicious passion for her who would
    be his wife —

This was the heart he offered — the upright life
    he gave —
This is the silent sermon of the patriot's nameless
    grave.

Shrine of a nation's honor — stone left blank for
    a name —

Light on the dark horizon to guide us clear from
    shame —

Chord struck deep with the keynote, telling us
    what can save —
"A nation among the nations," or forever a
    nameless grave.

Such is the will of the martyr — the burden we
    still must bear ;
But even from death he reaches the legacy to
    share :

He teaches the secret of manhood — the watch-
    word of those who aspire —
That men must follow freedom though it lead
    through blood and fire ;

That sacrifice is the bitter draught which freemen
    still must quaff —
That every patriotic life is the patriot's epitaph.

JOHN MITCHEL.

DIED MARCH 20, 1875.

I.

DEAD, with his harness on him:
  Rigid and cold and white,
Marking the place of the vanguard
  Still in the ancient fight.

The climber dead on the hill-side,
  Before the height is won:
The workman dead on the building,
  Before the work is done!

O, for a tongue to utter
  The words that should be said —
Of his worth that was silver, living,
  That is gold and jasper, dead!

Dead — but the death was fitting:
  His life, to the latest breath,
Was poured like wax on the chart of right,
  And is sealed by the stamp of Death!

Dead — but the end was fitting:
  First in the ranks he led;
And he marks the height of his nation's gain,
  As he lies in his harness — dead!

II.

Weep for him, Ireland — mother lonely;
  Weep for the son who died for thee.
Wayward he was, but he loved thee only,
  Loyal and fearless as son could be.
Weep for him, Ireland — sorrowing nation -
  Faithful to all who are true to thee:
Never a son in thy desolation
  Had holier love for thy cause than he.

Sons of the Old Land, mark the story —
  Mother and son in the final test :
Weeping she sits in her darkened glory,
  Holding her dead to her stricken breast.
Only the dead on her knees are lying —
  Ah, poor mother beneath the Cross !
Strength is won by the constant trying,
  Crowns are gemmed by the tears of loss !

Sons of the Old Land, mark the story —
  Mother and son to each other true :
She called, and he answered, old and hoary,
  And gave her his life as a man should do.
She may weep — but for us no weeping :
  Tears are vain till the work is done ;
Tears for her — but for us the keeping
  Our hearts as true as her faithful son.

A NATION'S TEST.

READ AT THE O'CONNELL CENTENNIAL IN BOSTON, ON
AUGUST 6, 1875.

I.

A NATION'S greatness lies in men, not
    acres ;
One master-mind is worth a million hands.
No royal robes have marked the planet-shakers,
    But Samson-strength to burst the ages' bands.
The might of empire gives no crown supernal —
    Athens is here — but where is Macedon ?
A dozen lives make Greece and Rome eternal,
    And England's fame might safely rest on one.

Here test and text are drawn from Nature's
        preaching :
    Afric and Asia — half the rounded earth —
In teeming lives the solemn truth are teaching,
    That insect-millions may have human birth.

Sun-kissed and fruitful, every clod is breeding
  A petty life, too small to reach the eye:
So must it be, with no Man thinking, leading,
  The generations creep their course and die.

Hapless the lands, and doomed amid the races,
  That give no answer to this royal test;
Their toiling tribes will droop ignoble faces,
  Till earth in pity takes them back to rest.
A vast monotony may not be evil,
  But God's light tells us it cannot be good;
Valley and hill have beauty — but the level
  Must bear a shadeless and a stagnant brood.

II.

I bring the touchstone, Motherland, to thee,
  And test thee trembling, fearing thou shouldst
      fail;
If fruitless, sonless, thou wert proved to be,
  Ah, what would love and memory avail?

Brave land! God has blest thee!
Thy strong heart I feel,
As I touch thee and test thee —
Dear land!   As the steel
To the magnet flies upward, so rises thy breast,
With a motherly pride to the touch of the test.

III.

See! she smiles beneath the touchstone, looking
    on her distant youth,
Looking down her line of leaders and of workers
    for the truth.
Ere the Teuton, Norseman, Briton, left the
    primal woodland spring,
When their rule was might and rapine, and their
    law a painted king;
When the sun of art and learning still was in the
    Orient;
When the pride of Babylonia under Cyrus' hand
    was shent;

When the sphinx's introverted eye turned fresh
    from Egypt's guilt;

When the Persian bowed to Athens; when the
    Parthenon was built;

When the Macedonian climax closed the Com-
    monwealths of Greece;

When the wrath of Roman manhood burst on
    Tarquin for Lucrece —

Then was Erin rich in knowledge — thence from
    out her Ollamh's store —

Kenned to-day by students only — grew her
    ancient *Senchus More;* *

Then were reared her mighty builders, who made
    temples to the sun —

There they stand — the old Round Towers —
    showing how their work was done:

---

* "Senchus More," or *Great Law*, the title of the Brehon
Laws, translated by O'Donovan and O'Curry. Ollamh Fola,
who reigned 900 years B.C., organized a triennial parliament
at Tara, of the chiefs, priests, and bards, who digested the
laws into a record called the Psalter of Tara. Ollamh Fola
founded schools of history, medicine, philosophy, poetry, and
astronomy, which were protected by his successors. Kimbath
(450 B.C.) and Hugony (300 B.C.) also promoted the civil
interests of the kingdom in a remarkable manner.

Thrice a thousand years upon them — shaming all
  our later art —
Warning fingers raised to tell us we must build
  with rev'rent heart.

Ah, we call thee Mother Erin! Mother thou in
  right of years;
Mother in the large fruition — mother in the joys
  and tears.
All thy life has been a symbol — we can only
  read a part:
God will flood thee yet with sunshine for the
  woes that drench thy heart.
All thy life has been symbolic of a human
  mother's life:
Youth's sweet hopes and dreams have vanished,
  and the travail and the strife
Are upon thee in the present; but thy work until
  to-day
Still has been for truth and manhood — and it
  shall not pass away:

Justice lives, though judgment lingers — angels'
    feet are heavy shod —
But a planet's years are moments in th' eternal
    day of God !

IV.

Out from the valley of death and tears,
From the war and want of a thousand years,
From the mark of sword and the rust of chain,
From the smoke and blood of the penal laws,
The Irish men and the Irish cause
Come out in the front of the field again !

What says the stranger to such a vitality?
What says the statesman to this nationality?
Flung on the shore of a sea of defeat,
Hardly the swimmers have sprung to their feet,
When the nations are thrilled by a clarion-word,
And Burke, the philosopher-statesman, is heard.

When shall his equal be? Down from the stellar
    height
Sees he the planet and all on its girth —
India, Columbia, and Europe — his eagle-sight
    Sweeps at a glance all the wrong upon earth.
Races or sects were to him a profanity :
    Hindoo and Negro and Kelt were as one ;
Large as mankind was his splendid humanity,
    Large in its record the work he has done.

V.

What need to mention men of minor note,
    When there be minds that all the heights
    attain ?
What school-boy knoweth not the hand that wrote
    "Sweet Auburn, loveliest village of the plain" ?
What man that speaketh English e'er can lift
    His voice 'mid scholars, who hath missed the lore
Of Berkeley, Curran, Sheridan, and Swift,
    The art of Foley and the songs of Moore?

Grattan and Flood and Emmet — where is he
   That hath not learned respect for such as these?
Who loveth humor, and hath yet to see
   Lover and Prout and Lever and Maclise?

VI.

Great men grow greater by the lapse of time:
   We know those least whom we have seen the
      latest;
And they, 'mongst those whose **names** have
   grown sublime,
Who worked for Human Liberty, are greatest.

And now for one who allied will to work,
   And thought to act, and burning speech to
      thought;
Who gained the prizes that were seen by
   Burke —
   Burke felt the wrong — O'Connell felt, and
      fought.

Ever the same — from boyhood up to death:
  His race was crushed — his people were
      defamed;
He found the spark, and fanned it with his
      breath,
  And fed the fire, till all the nation flamed!

He roused the farms — he made the serf a
      yeoman;
  He drilled his millions and he faced the foe;
But not with lead or steel he struck the foeman:
  Reason the sword — and human right the blow.

He fought for home — but no land-limit bounded
  O'Connell's faith, nor curbed his sympathies;
All wrong to liberty must be confounded,
  Till men were chainless as the winds and seas.

He fought for faith — but with no narrow spirit;
  With ceaseless hand the bigot laws he smote;
One chart, he said, all mankind should inherit, —
  The right to worship and the right to vote.

Always the same — but yet a glinting prism:
  In wit, law, statecraft, still a master-hand;
An "uncrowned king," whose people's love was
    chrism;
  His title — Liberator of his Land!

"His heart's in Rome, his spirit is in heaven" —
  So runs the old song that his people sing;
A tall Round Tower they builded in Glasnevin —
  Fit Irish headstone for an Irish king!

VII.

O Motherland! there is no cause to doubt thee:
  Thy mark is left on every shore to-day.
Though grief and wrong may cling like robes
    about thee,
  Thy motherhood will keep thee queen alway.
In faith and patience working, and believing
  Not power alone can make a noble state:

Whate'er the land, though all things else con-
    ceiving,
  Unless it breed great men, it is not great.
Go on, dear land, and midst the generations
  Send out strong men to cry the word aloud;
Thy niche is empty still amidst the nations —
  Go on in faith, and God must raise the cloud.

THE FLYING DUTCHMAN.

L ONG time ago, from Amsterdam a vessel sailed
away, —
As fair a ship as ever flung aside the laughing
spray.
Upon the shore were tearful eyes, and scarfs were
in the air,
As to her, o'er the Zuyder Zee, went fond adieu
and prayer;
And brave hearts, yearning shoreward from the
outward-going ship,
Felt lingering kisses clinging still to tear-wet cheek
and lip.
She steered for some far eastern clime, and, as she
skimmed the seas,
Each taper mast was bending like a rod before the
breeze.

Her captain was a stalwart man, — an iron heart
    had he. —
From childhood's days he sailed upon the rolling
    Zuyder Zee:
He nothing feared upon the earth, and scarcely
    heaven feared,
He would have dared and done whatever mortal
    man had dared!
He looked aloft, where high in air the pennant cut
    the blue,
And every rope and spar and sail was firm and
    strong and true.
He turned him from the swelling sail to gaze upon
    the shore, —
Ah! little thought the skipper then 'twould meet
    his eye no more:
He dreamt not that an awful doom was hanging
    o'er his ship,
That Vanderdecken's name would yet make pale
    the speaker's lip.
The vessel bounded on her way, and spire and
    dome went down, —

Ere darkness fell, beneath the wave had sunk the
    distant town.

No more, no more, ye hapless crew, shall Holland
    meet your eye.

In lingering hope and keen suspense, maid, wife,
    and child shall die !

Away, away the vessel speeds, till sea and sky
    alone

Are round her, as her course she steers across the
    torrid zone.

Away, until the North Star fades, the Southern
    Cross is high,

And myriad gems of brightest beam are sparkling
    in the sky.

The tropic winds are left behind ; she nears the
    Cape of Storms,

Where awful Tempest ever sits enthroned in wild
    alarms ;

Where Ocean in his anger shakes aloft his foamy
    crest,

Disdainful of the weakly toys that ride upon his
    breast.

Fierce swell the winds and waters round the Dutchman's gallant ship,

But, to their rage, defiance rings from Vanderdecken's lip :

Impotent they to make him swerve, their might he
dares despise,

As straight he holds his onward course, and wind
and wave defies.

For days and nights he struggles in the wierd,
unearthly fight.

His brow is bent, his eye is fierce, but looks of deep
affright

Amongst the mariners go round, as hopelessly they
steer :

They do not dare to murmur, but they whisper
what they fear.

Their black-browed captain awes them : 'neath his
darkened eye they quail,

And in a grim and sullen mood their bitter fate
bewail.

As some fierce rider ruthless spurs a timid, wavering horse,

He drives his shapely vessel, and they watch the
    reckless course,
Till once again their skipper's laugh is flung upon
    the blast:
The placid ocean smiles beyond, the dreaded Cape
    is passed!

Away across the Indian main the vessel northward
    glides;
A thousand murmuring ripples break along her
    graceful sides:
The perfumed breezes fill her sails, — her destined
    port she nears, —
The captain's brow has lost its frown, the mariners
    their fears.
"Land ho!" at length the welcome sound the
    watchful sailor sings,
And soon within an Indian bay the ship at anchor
    swings.
Not idle then the busy crew: ere long the spacious
    hold
Is emptied of its western freight, and stored with
    silk and gold.

Again the ponderous anchor's weighed; the shore
    is left behind,
The snowy sails are bosomed out before the favor-
    ing wind.
Across the warm blue Indian sea the vessel south-
    ward flies,
And once again the North Star fades and Austral
    beacons rise.
For home she steers! she seems to know and
    answer to the word,
And swifter skims the burnished deep, like some
    fair ocean-bird.
"For home! for home!" the merry crew with
    gladsome voices cry,
And dark-browed Vanderdecken has a mild light
    in his eye.

But once again the Cape draws near, and furious
    billows rise ;
And still the daring Dutchman's laugh the hurri-
    cane defies.
But wildly shrieked the tempest ere the scornful
    sound had died,

A warning to the daring man to curb his impious
    pride.
A crested mountain struck the ship, and like a
    frighted bird
She trembled 'neath the awful shock. Then Van-
    derdecken heard
A pleading voice within the gale, — his better an-
    gel spoke,
But fled before his scowling look, as mast-high
    mountains broke
Around the trembling vessel, till the crew with
    terror paled;
But Vanderdecken never flinched, nor 'neath the
    thunders quailed.
With folded arms and stern-pressed lips, dark anger
    in his eye,
He answered back the threatening frown that
    lowered o'er the sky.
With fierce defiance in his heart, and scornful look
    of flame,
He spoke, and thus with impious voice blasphemed
    God's holy name: —

"Howl on, ye winds! ye tempests, howl! your
    rage is spent in vain :
Despite your strength, your frowns, your hate, I 'll
    ride upon the main.
Defiance to your idle shrieks!   I 'll sail upon my
    path :
I cringe not for thy Maker's smile, — I care not for
    His wrath!"

He ceased.   An awful silence fell: the tempest
    and the sea
Were hushed in sudden stillness by the Ruler's
    dread decree.
The ship was riding motionless within the gather-
    ing gloom ;
The Dutchman stood upon the poop and heard his
    dreadful doom.
The hapless crew were on the deck in swooning
    terror prone, —
They, too, were bound in fearful fate. In angered
    thunder-tone

The judgment words swept o'er the sea: "Go,
    wretch, accurst, condemned!

Go sail for ever on the deep, by shrieking tempests
    hemmed.

No home, no port, no calm, no rest, no gentle
    fav'ring breeze,

Shall ever greet thee. Go, accurst! and battle
    with the seas!

Go, braggart! struggle with the storm, nor ever
    cease to live,

But bear a million times the pangs that death and
    fear can give.

Away! and hide thy guilty head, a curse to all thy
    kind

Who ever see thee struggling, wretch, with ocean
    and with wind.

Away, presumptuous worm of earth! Go teach
    thy fellow-worms

The awful fate that waits on him who braves the
    King of Storms!"

'Twas o'er.   A lurid lightning flash lit up the sea
  and sky
Around and o'er the fated ship; then rose a wailing cry
From every heart within her, of keen anguish and
  despair;
But mercy was for them no more, — it died away
  in air.

Once more the lurid light gleamed out, — the ship
  was still at rest,
The crew were standing at their posts; with arms
  across his breast
Still stood the captain on the poop, but bent and
  crouching now
He bowed beneath that fiat dread, and o'er his
  swarthy brow
Swept lines of anguish, as if he a thousand years
  of pain
Had lived and suffered.   Then across the heaving,
  angry main

The tempest shrieked triumphant, and the augry
    waters hissed

Their vengeful hate against the toy they oftentimes
    had kissed.

And ever through the midnight storm that hapless
    crew must speed:

They try to round the stormy Cape, but never can
    succeed.

And oft when gales are wildest, and the lightning's
    vivid sheen

Flashes back the ocean's anger, still the Phantom
    Ship is seen

Ever sailing to the southward in the fierce tor-
    nado's swoop,

With her ghostly crew and canvas, and her captain
    on the poop,

Unrelenting, unforgiven; and 'tis said that every
    word

Of his blasphemous defiance still upon the gale is
    heard !

But Heaven help the ship near which the dismal
    sailor steers, —

The doom of those is sealed to whom that Phantom Ship appears:

They 'll never reach their destined port, — they 'll
see their homes no more, —

They who see the Flying Dutchman — never,
never reach the shore!

UNCLE NED'S TALE.

AN OLD DRAGOON'S STORY.

I OFTEN, musing, wander back to days long
    since gone by,
And far-off scenes and long-lost forms arise to
    fancy's eye.
A group familiar now I see, who all but one are
    fled, —
My mother, sister Jane, myself, and dear old Uncle
    Ned.
I 'll tell you how I see them now.   First, mother
    in her chair
Sits knitting by the parlor fire, with anxious matron
    air ;
My sister Jane, just nine years old, is seated at her
    feet,
With look demure, as if she, too, were thinking
    how to meet

The butcher's or the baker's bill,—though not a
    thought has she
Of aught beside her girlish toys; and next to her
    I see
Myself, a sturdy lad of twelve,—neglectful of the
    book
That open lies upon my knee,—my fixed admir-
    ing look
At Uncle Ned, upon the left, whose upright, mar-
    tial mien,
Whose empty sleeve and gray moustache, proclaim
    what he has been.
My mother I had always loved; my father then
    was dead;
But 'twas more than love—'twas worship—I felt
    for Uncle Ned.
Such tales he had of battle-fields,—the victory
    and the rout,
The ringing cheer, the dying shriek, the loud
    exulting shout!
And how, forgetting age and wounds, his eye
    would kindle bright,

When telling of some desperate ride or close and
    deadly fight!

But oft I noticed, in the midst of some wild martial
    tale,

To which I lent attentive ear, my mother's cheek
    grow pale:

She sighed to see my kindled look, and feared I
    might be led

To follow in the wayward steps of poor old Uncle
    Ned.

But with all the wondrous tales he told, 'twas
    strange I never heard

Of his last fight, for of that day he never spoke a
    word.

And yet 'twas there he lost his arm, and once he
    e'en confessed

'Twas there he won the glittering cross he wore
    upon his breast.

It hung the centre of a group of Glory's emblems
    fair,

And royal hands, he told me once, had placed the
    bauble there.

Each day that passed I hungered more to hear
    about that fight,
And oftentimes I prayed in vain. At length, one
    winter's night, —
The very night I speak of now, — with more than
    usual care
I filled his pipe, then took my stand beside my
    uncle's chair:
I fixed my eyes upon the Cross, — he saw my youth-
    ful plan ;
And, smiling, laid the pipe aside and thus the tale
    began : —

" Well, boy, it was in summer time, and just at
    morning's light
We heard the ' Boot and Saddle !' sound: the foe
    was then in sight,
Just winding round a distant hill and opening on
    the plain.
Each trooper looked with careful eye to girth and
    curb and rein.

We snatched a hasty breakfast, — we were old
    campaigners then:
That morn, of all our splendid corps, we 'd scarce
    one hundred men;
But they were soldiers, tried and true, who 'd
    rather die than yield:
The rest were scattered far and wide o'er many a
    hard-fought field.
Our trumpet now rang sharply out, and at a
    swinging pace
We left the bivouac behind; and soon the eye
    could trace
The columns moving o'er the plain. Oh! 'twas a
    stirring sight
To see two mighty armies there preparing for the
    fight:
To watch the heavy masses, as, with practised,
    steady wheel,
They opened out in slender lines of brightly flash-
    ing steel.
Our place was on the farther flank, behind some
    rising ground,

That hid the stirring scene from view; but soon a
    booming sound
Proclaimed the opening of the fight.   Then war's
    loud thunder rolled,
And hurtling shells and whistling balls their deadly
    message told.
We hoped to have a gallant day; our hearts were
    all aglow;
We longed for one wild, sweeping charge, to chase
    the flying foe.
Our troopers marked the hours glide by, but still
    no orders came:
They clutched their swords, and muttered words
    'twere better not to name.
For hours the loud artillery roared, — the sun was
    at its height, —
Still there we lay behind that hill, shut out from
    all the fight!
We heard the maddened charging yells, the ringing
    British cheers,
And all the din of glorious war kept sounding in
    our ears.

Our hearts with fierce impatience throbbed, we
    cursed the very hill
That hid the sight: the evening fell, and we were
    idle still.
The horses, too, were almost wild, and told with
    angry snort
And blazing eye their fierce desire to join the
    savage sport.
When lower still the sun had sunk, and with it
    all our hope,
A horseman, soiled with smoke and sweat, came
    dashing down the slope.
He bore the wished-for orders. 'At last!' our
    Colonel cried;
And as he read the brief despatch his glance was
    filled with pride.
Then he who bore the orders, in a low, emphatic
    tone,
The stern, expressive sentence spoke, — '*He said it
    must be done!*'
'It *shall* be done!' our Colonel cried. 'Men, look
    to strap and girth,

We 've work to do this day will prove what every
    man is worth ;

Ay, work, my lads, will make amends for all our
    long delay, —

The General says on us depends the fortune of the
    day ! '

" No order needed we to mount, — each man was
    in his place,

And stern and dangerous was the look on every
    veteran face.

We trotted sharply up the hill, and halted on the
    brow,

And then that glorious field appeared.   Oh ! lad,
    I see it now !

But little time had we to spare for idle gazing then :

Beneath us, in the valley, stood a dark-clad mass of
    men :

It cut the British line in two.   Our Colonel shouted,
    ' There !

Behold your work !   Our orders are *to charge and
break that square !* '

Each trooper drew a heavy breath, then gathered
    up his reins,
And pressed the helmet o'er his brow ; the horses
    tossed their manes
In protest fierce against the curb, and spurned the
    springy heath,
Impatient for the trumpet's sound to bid them rush
    to death.

" Well, boy, that moment seemed an hour : at last
    we heard the words, —
' Dragoons ! I know you 'll follow me. Ride steady,
    men ! Draw swords !'
The trumpet sounded : off we dashed, at first with
    steady pace,
But growing swifter as we went. Oh ! 'twas a
    gallant race !
Three-fourths the ground was left behind : the loud
    and thrilling ' Charge !'
Rang out ; but, fairly frantic now, we needed not
    to urge

With voice or rein our gallant steeds, or touch
 their foaming flanks.
They seemed to fly. Now straight in front appeared
 the kneeling ranks.
Above them waved a standard broad : we saw their
 rifles raised, —
A moment more, with awful crash, the deadly
 volley blazed.
The bullets whistled through our ranks, and many
 a trooper fell ;
But we were left. What cared we then ? but onward rushing still !
Again the crash roared fiercely out; but on ! still
 madly on !
We heard the shrieks of dying men, but recked not
 who was gone.
We gored the horses' foaming flanks, and on through
 smoke and glare
We wildly dashed, with clenchéd teeth. We had
 no thought, no care !
Then came a sudden, sweeping rush. Again with
 savage heel

I struck my horse: with awful bound he rose right
    o'er their steel!

"Well, boy, I cannot tell you how that dreadful
    leap was made,
But there I rode, inside the square, and grasped a
    reeking blade.
I cared not that I was alone, my eyes seem filled
    with blood:
I never thought a man could feel in such a mur-
    derous mood.
I parried not, nor guarded thrusts; I felt not pain
    or wound,
But madly spurred the frantic horse, and swept my
    sword around.
I tried to reach the standard sheet; but there at
    last was foiled.
The gallant horse was jaded now, and from the
    steel recoiled.
They saw his fright, and pressed him then: his
    terror made him rear,
And falling back he crushed their ranks, and broke
    their guarded square!

My comrades saw the gap he made, and soon came
      `dashing in ;

They raised me up, — I felt no hurt, but mingled
      in the din.

I'd seen some fearful work before, but never was
      engaged

In such a wild and savage fight as now around me
      raged.

The foe had ceased their firing, and now plied the
      deadly steel :

Though all our men were wounded then, no pain
      they seemed to feel.

No groans escaped from those who fell, but horrid
      oaths instead,

And scowling looks of hate were on the features
      of the dead.

The fight was round the standard : though outnum-
      bered ten to one,

We held our ground, — ay, more than that, — we
      still kept pushing on.

Our men now made a desperate rush to take the
      flag by storm.

I seized the pole, a blow came down and crushed
    my outstretched arm.
I felt a sudden thrill of pain, but that soon passed
    away;
And, with a devilish thirst for blood, again I joined
    the fray.
At last we rallied all our strength, and charged o'er
    heaps of slain:
Some fought to death; some wavered, — then fled
    across the plain.

" Well, boy, the rest is all confused: there was a
    fearful rout;
I saw our troopers chase the foe, and heard their
    maddened shout.
Then came a blank: my senses reeled, I know not
    how I fell;
I seemed to grapple with a foe, but that I cannot
    tell.
My mind was gone: when it came back I saw the
    moon on high;
Around me all was still as death. I gazed up at
    the sky,

And watched the glimmering stars above, — so
quiet did they seem, —
And all that dreadful field appeared like some wild,
fearful dream.
But memory soon came back again, and cleared my
wandering brain,
And then from every joint and limb shot fiery darts
of pain.
My throat was parched, the burning thirst increased
with every breath ;
I made no effort to arise, but wished and prayed for
death.
My bridle arm was broken, and lay throbbing on
the sward,
But something still my right hand grasped : I
thought it was my sword.
I raised my hand to cast it off, — no reeking blade
was there ;
Then life and strength returned, — I held the
Standard of the Square !
With bounding heart I gained my feet.   Oh ! then
I wished to live,

'Twas strange the strength and love of life that
    standard seemed to give!
I gazed around: far down the vale I saw a camp-
    fire's glow.
With wandering step I ran that way, — I recked
    not friend or foe.
Though stumbling now o'er heaps of dead, now
    o'er a stiffened horse,
I heeded not, but watched the light, and held my
    onward course.
But soon that flash of strength had failed, and
    checked my feverish speed;
Again my throat was all ablaze, my wounds began
    to bleed.
I knew that if I fell again, my chance of life was
    gone,
So, leaning on the standard-pole, I still kept strug-
    gling on.
At length I neared the camp-fire: there were scar-
    let jackets round,
And swords and brazen helmets lay strewn upon
    the ground.

Some distance off, in order ranged, stood men, —
 about a score :

O God! 'twas all that now remained of my old
 gallant corps!

The muster-roll was being called : to every well-
 known name

I heard the solemn answer, — ' Dead ! '   At length
 my own turn came.

I paused to hear, — a comrade answered, ' Dead !
 I saw him fall ! '

I could not move another step, I tried in vain to call.

My life was flowing fast, and all around was gathering haze,

And o'er the heather tops I watched my comrades'
 cheerful blaze.

I thought such anguish as I felt was more than man
 could bear.

O God! it was an awful thing to die with help so
 near !

And death was stealing o'er me : with the strength
 of wild despair

I raised the standard o'er my head, and waved it
 through the air.

Then all grew dim: the fire, the men, all vanished
    from my sight,
My senses reeled; I know no more of that eventful
    night.
'Twas weeks before my mind came back: I knew
    not where I lay,
But kindly hands were round me, and old comrades
    came each day.
They told me how the waving flag that night had
    caught their eye,
And how they found me bleeding there, and thought
    that I must die;
They brought me all the cheering news, — the war
    was at an end.
No wonder 'twas, with all their care, I soon began
    to mend.
The General came to see me, too, with all his bril-
    liant train,
But what he said, or how I felt, to tell you now
    'twere vain.
Enough, I soon grew strong again: the wished-for
    route had come,

And all the gallant veteran troops set out with
cheers for home.

We soon arrived; and then, my lad, 'twould thrill
your heart to hear

How England welcomed home her sons with many
a ringing cheer.

But tush! what boots it now to speak of what was
said or done?

The victory was dearly bought, our bravest hearts
were gone.

Ere long the King reviewed us. Ah! that memory
is sweet!

They made me bear the foreign flag, and lay it at
his feet.

I parted from my brave old corps: 'twere matter,
lad, for tears,

To leave the kind old comrades I had ridden with
for years.

I was no longer fit for war, my wanderings had to
cease.

There, boy, I've told you all my tales. Now let
me smoke in peace."

How vivid grows the picture now! how bright
    each scene appears!
I trace each loved and long-lost face with eyes be-
    dimmed in tears.
How plain I hear thee, Uncle Ned, and see thy
    musing look,
Comparing all thy glory to the curling wreaths of
    smoke!
A truer, braver soldier ne'er for king and country
    bled.
His wanderings are for ever o'er. God rest thee,
    Uncle Ned!

UNCLE NED'S TALES.

HOW THE FLAG WAS SAVED.*

'TWAS a dismal winter's evening, fast without
    came down the snow,
But within, the cheerful fire cast a ruddy, genial
    glow
O'er our pleasant little parlor, that was then my
    mother's pride.
There she sat beside the glowing grate, my sister
    by her side ;
And beyond, within the shadow, in a cosy little
    nook
Uncle Ned and I were sitting, and in whispering
    tones we spoke.
I was asking for a story he had promised me to
    tell,—

* An incident from the record of the Enniskillen Dragoons in
Spain, under General Picton.

Of his comrade, old Dick Hilton, how he fought
    and how he fell;

And with eager voice I pressed him, till a mighty
    final cloud

Blew he slowly, then upon his breast his grisly
    head he bowed,

And, musing, stroked his gray mustache ere he
    began to speak,

Then brushed a tear that stole along his bronzed
    and furrowed cheek.

"Ah, no! I will not speak to-night of that sad
    tale," he cried:

"Some other time I'll tell you, boy, about that
    splendid ride.

Your words have set me thinking of the many care-
    less years

That comrade rode beside me, and have caused
    these bitter tears;

For I loved him, boy, — for twenty years we gal-
    loped rein to rein, —

In peace and war, through all that time, **stanch**
    comrades had we been.

As boys we rode together when our soldiering **first**
    began,
And in all those years I knew him for a true and
    trusty man.
One who never swerved from danger, — for he knew
    not how to fear, —
If grim Death arrayed his legions, Dick would
    charge him with a cheer.
He was happiest in a struggle or a wild and dan-
    gerous ride :
Every inch a trooper was he, and he cared **for**
    naught beside.
He was known for many a gallant deed : to-night
    I 'll tell you one,
And no braver feat of arms was by a soldier ever
    done.
'Twas when we were young and fearless, for 'twas
    in our first campaign,
When we galloped through the orange groves and
    fields of sunny Spain.
Our wary old commander was retiring from the
    foe,

Who came pressing close upon us, with a proud,
    exulting show.
We could hear their taunting laughter, and within
    our very sight
Did they ride defiant round us, — ay, and dared us
    to the fight.
But brave old Picton heeded not, but held his
    backward track,
And smiling said the day would come to pay the
    Frenchmen back.
And come it did: one morning, long before the
    break of day,
We were standing to our arms, all ready for the
    coming fray.
Soon the sun poured down his glory on the hostile
    lines arrayed,
And his beams went flashing brightly back from
    many a burnished blade,
Soon to change its spotless lustre for a reeking
    crimson stain,
In some heart, then throbbing proudly, that will
    never throb again

When that sun has reached his zenith, life and
    pride will then have fled,
And his beams will mock in splendor o'er the
    ghastly heaps of dead.
Oh, 'tis sad to think how many —— but I wander,
    lad, I fear ;
And, though the moral's good, I guess the tale
    you'd rather hear.
Well, I said that we were ready, and the foe was
    ready, too ;
Soon the fight was raging fiercely, — thick and fast
    the bullets flew,
With a bitter hiss of malice, as if hungry for the
    life
To be torn from manly bosoms in the maddening
    heat of strife.
Distant batteries were thundering, pouring grape
    and shell like rain,
And the cruel missiles hurtled with their load of
    death and pain,
Which they carried, like fell demons, to the heart
    of some brigade,

Where the sudden, awful stillness told the havoc
    they had made.
Thus the struggle raged till noon, and neither side
    could vantage show;
Then the tide of battle turned, and swept in favor
    of the foe!
Fiercer still the cannon thundered, — wilder
    screamed the grape and shell, —
Onward pressed the French battalions, — back the
    British masses fell!
Then, as on its prey devoted, fierce the hungered
    vulture swoops,
Swung the foeman's charging squadrons down upon
    our broken troops.
Victory hovered o'er their standard, — on they
    swept with maddened shout,
Spreading death and havoc round them, till retreat
    was changed to rout!
'Twas a saddening sight to witness; and, when
    Picton saw them fly,
Grief and shame were mixed and burning in the
    old commander's eye.

We were riding in his escort, close behind him, on
    a height
Which the fatal field commanded; thence we
    viewed the growing flight.

"But, my lad, I now must tell you something more
    about that hill,
And I'll try to make you see the spot as I can see
    it still.
Right before us, o'er the battle-field, the fall was
    sheer and steep;
On our left the ground fell sloping, in a pleasant,
    grassy sweep,
Where the aides went dashing swiftly, bearing
    orders to and fro,
For by that sloping side alone they reached the
    plain below.
On our right — now pay attention, boy — a yawn-
    ing fissure lay,
As if an earthquake's shock had split the moun-
    tain's side away.
And in the dismal gulf, far down, we heard the
    angry roar

Of a foaming mountain torrent, that, mayhap, the
    cleft had wore,

As it rushed for countless ages through its black
    and secret lair;

But no matter how 'twas formed, my lad, the
    yawning gulf was there.

And from the farther side a stone projected o'er the
    gorge, —

'Twas strange to see the massive rock just balanced
    on the verge;

It seemed as if an eagle's weight the ponderous
    mass of stone

Would topple from its giddy height, and send it
    crashing down.

It stretched far o'er the dark abyss; but, though
    'twere footing good,

'Twas twenty feet or more from off the side on
    which we stood.

Beyond the cleft a gentle slope went down and
    joined the plain, —

Now, lad, back to where we halted, and again
    resume the rein.

I said our troops were routed.   Far and near **they**
    broke and fled,
The grape-shot tearing through them, leaving lanes
    of mangled dead.
All order lost, they left the fight, — they threw
    their arms away,
And joined in one wild panic rout, — ah! 'twas a
    bitter day!

" But did I say that *all* was lost?   Nay, one brave
    corps stood fast,
Determined they would never fly, but fight it to
    the last.
They barred the Frenchman from his prey, and
    his whole fury braved, —
One brief hour could they hold their ground, **the**
    army might be saved.
Fresh troops were hurrying to our aid, — we **saw**
    their glittering head, —
Ah, God! how those brave hearts were raked by
    the death-shower of lead!
But stand they did : they never flinched nor **took**
    one backward stride,

They sent their bayonets home, and then with
    stubborn courage died.

But few were left of that brave band when the
    dread hour had passed,

Still, faint and few, they held their flag above them
    to the last.

But now a cloud of horsemen, like a shadowy
    avalanche,

Sweeps down: as Picton sees them, e'en his cheek
    is seen to blanch.

They were not awed, that little band, but rallied
    once again,

And sent us back a farewell cheer. Then burst
    from reckless men

The anguished cry, 'God help them!' as we saw
    the feeble flash

Of their last defiant volley, when upon them with
    a crash

Burst the gleaming lines of riders, — one by one
    they disappear,

And the chargers' hoofs are trampling on the last
    of that brave square!

On swept the squadrons! Then we looked where
    last the band was seen:
A scarlet heap was all that marked the place where
    they had been!
Still forward spurred the horsemen, eager to com
    plete the rout;
But our lines had been re-formed now, and five
    thousand guns belched out
A reception to the squadrons, — rank on rank was
    piled that day,
Every bullet hissed out 'Vengeance!' as it whis-
    tled on its way.

" And now it was, with maddened hearts, we saw
    a galling sight:
A French hussar was riding close beneath us on
    . the right, —
He held a British standard!   With insulting shout
    he stood,
And waved the flag, — its heavy folds drooped
    down with shame and blood, —
The blood of hearts unconquered: 'twas the flag
    of the stanch corps

That had fought to death beneath it, — it was heavy
  with their gore.

The foreign dog! I see him as he holds the
  standard down,

And makes his charger trample on its colors and
  its crown!

But his life soon paid the forfeit: with a cry of
  rage and pain,

Hilton dashes from the escort, like a tiger from his
  chain.

Nought he sees but that insulter; and he strikes
  his frightened horse

With his clenchéd hand, and spurs him, with a
  bitter-spoken curse,

Straight as bullet from a rifle — but, great Lord!
  he has not seen,

In his angry thirst for vengeance, the black gulf
  that lies between!

All our warning shouts unheeded, starkly on he
  headlong rides,

And lifts his horse, with bloody spurs deep buried
  in his sides.

God's mercy! does he see the gulf?   Ha! now his
    purpose dawns
Upon our minds, as nearer still the rocky fissure
    yawns:
Where from the farther side the stone leans o'er
    the stream beneath,
He means to take the awful leap! Cold horror
    checks our breath,
And still and mute we watch him now: he nears
    the fearful place ;
We hear him shout to cheer the horse, and keep
    the headlong pace.
Then comes a rush, — short strides, — a blow! —
    the horse bounds wildly on,
Springs high in air o'er the abyss, and lands
    upon the stone!
It trembles, topples 'neath their weight! it sinks!
    ha! bravely done!
Another spring, — they gain the side, — the pon-
    derous rock is gone
With crashing roar, a thousand feet, down to the
    flood below,

And Hilton, heedless of its noise, is riding at the
    foe !

" The Frenchman stared in wonder : he was brave,
    and would not run,
'Twould merit but a coward's brand to turn and
    fly from one.
But still he shuddered at the glance from 'neath
    that knitted brow :
He knew 'twould be a death fight, but there was
    no shrinking now.
He pressed his horse to meet the shock : straight at
    him Hilton made,
And as they closed the Frenchman's cut fell harm-
    less on his blade ;
But scarce a moment's time had passed ere, spur-
    ring from the field,
A troop of cuirassiers closed round and called on
    him to yield.
One glance of scorn he threw them, — all his answer
    in a frown, —
And riding at their leader with one sweep he cut
    him down ;

Then aimed at him who held the flag a cut of
 crushing might,
And split him to the very chin!—a horrid, ghastly
 sight!
He seized the standard from his hand; but now
 the Frenchmen close,
And that stout soldier, all alone, fights with a
 hundred foes!
They cut and cursed,—a dozen swords were whistling round his head;
He could not guard on every side,—from fifty
 wounds he bled.
His sabre crashed through helm and blade, as
 though it were a mace;
He cut their steel cuirasses and he slashed them
 o'er the face.
One tall dragoon closed on him, but he wheeled
 his horse around,
And cloven through the helmet went the trooper
 to the ground.
But his sabre blade was broken by the fury of the
 blow,

And he hurled the useless, bloody hilt against the
    nearest foe ;
Then furled the colors round the pole, and, like a
    levelled lance,
He charged with that red standard through the
    bravest troops of France!
His horse, as lion-hearted, scarcely needed to be
    urged,
And steed and rider bit the dust before him as he
    charged.
Straight on he rode, and down they went, till he
    had cleared the ranks,
Then once again he loosed the rein and struck his
    horse's flanks.
A cheer broke from the French dragoons, — a loud,
    admiring shout ! —
As off he rode, and o'er him shook the tattered
    colors out.
Still might they ride him down : they scorned to fire
    or to pursue, —
Brave hearts ! they cheered him to our lines, —
    their army cheering, too !

And we — what did we do? you ask.   Well, boy,
    we did not cheer,

Nor not one sound of welcome reached our hero
    comrade's ear ;

But, as he rode along the ranks, each soldier's head
    was bare, —

Our hearts were far too full for cheers, — we wel-
    comed him with prayer.

Ah! boy, we loved that dear old flag, — ay, loved
    it so, we cried

Like children, as we saw it wave in all its tattered
    pride!

No, boy, no cheers to greet him, though he played
    a noble part, —

We only prayed ' God bless him!' but that prayer
    came from the heart.

He knew we loved him for it, — he could see it in
    our tears, —

And such silent earnest love as that is better, boy,
    than cheers.

Next day we fought the Frenchman, and we drove
    him back, of course,

Though we lost some goodly soldiers, and old Picton lost a horse.
But there I've said enough: your mother's warning finger shook, —
Mind, never be a soldier, boy! — now let me have
   a smoke."

HAUNTED BY TIGERS.

NATHAN BEANS and William Lambert were
    two wild New England boys,
Known from infancy to revel only in forbidden
    joys.
Many a mother of Nantucket bristled when she
    heard them come,
With a horrid skulking whistle, tempting her good
    lad from home.
But for all maternal bristling little did they seem to
    care,
And they loved each other dearly, did this good-for-
    nothing pair.

So they lived till eighteen summers found them in
    the same repute, —
They had well-developed muscles, and loose char-
    acters to boot.

Then they did what wild Nantucket boys have
    never failed to do, —
Went and filled two oily bunks among a whaler's
    oily crew.
And the mothers, — ah! they raised their hands
    and blessed the lucky day,
While Nantucket waved its handkerchief to see
    them sail away.

On a four years' cruise they started in the brave old
    " Patience Parr,"
And were soon initiated in the mysteries of tar.
There they found the truth that whalers' tales are
    unsubstantial wiles, —
They were sick and sore and sorry ere they passed
    the Western Isles;
And their captain, old-man Sculpin, gave their
    fancies little scope,
For he argued with a marlinspike and reasoned
    with a rope.

But they stuck together bravely, they were Ish-
    maels with the crew:

Nathan's voice was never raised but Bill's support
      was uttered too ;

And whenever Beans was floored by Sculpin's cruel
      marlinspike,

Down beside him went poor Lambert, for his hand
      was clenched to strike.

So they passed two years in cruising, till one breath-
      less burning day

The old " Patience Parr " in Sunda Straits * with
      flapping canvas lay.

On her starboard side Sumatra's woods were dark
      beneath the glare,

And on her port stretched Java, slumbering in the
      yellow air, —

Slumbering as the jaguar slumbers, as the tropic
      ocean sleeps,

Smooth and smiling on its surface with a devil in
      its deeps.

So swooned Java's moveless forest, but the jungle
      round its root

---

* The Straits of Sunda, seven miles vide at the southern extremity, lie
between Sumatra and Java.

Knew the rustling anaconda and the tiger s padded
    foot.
There in Nature's rankest garden, Nature's worst
    alone is rife,
And a glorious land is wild-beast ruled for want of
    human life.
Scarce a harmless thing moved on it, not a living
    soul was near
From the frowning rocks of Java Head right north-
    ward to Anjier.
Crestless swells, like wind-raised canvas, made the
    whaler rise and dip,
Else she 'ay upon the water like a paralytic
    ship;
And beneath a topsail awning lay the lazy, languid
    crew,
Drinking in the precious coolness of the shadow,—
    all save two:
Two poor Ishmaels,—they were absent, Heaven
    help them!—roughly tied
'Neath the blistering cruel sun-glare in the fore-
    chains, side by side.

Side by side as it was always, each one with a
    word of cheer
For the other, and for his sake bravely choking
    back the tear.
Side by side, their pain or pastime never yet seemed
    good for one;
But whenever pain came, each in secret wished the
    other gone.

You who stop at home and saunter o'er your flower-
    scattered path,
With life's corners velvet-cushioned, have you seen
    a tyrant's wrath? —
Wrath, the rude and reckless demon, not the
    drawing-room display
Of an anger led by social lightning-rods upon its
    way.
Ah! my friends, wrath's raw materials on the land
    may sometimes be,
But the manufactured article is only found at sea.

And the wrath of old-man Sculpin was of texture
    Number One:

Never absent, — when the man smiled it was hid-
    den, but not gone.

Old church-members of Nantucket knew him for a
    shining lamp,

But his chronic Christian spirit was of pharisaic
    stamp.

When ashore, he prayed aloud of how he 'd sinned
    and been forgiven, —

How his evil ways had brought him 'thin an ace of
    losing heaven ;

Thank the Lord ! his eyes were opened, and so on ;
    but when the ship

Was just ready for a voyage, you could see old
    Sculpin's lip

Have a sort of nervous tremble, like a carter's long-
    leashed whip

Ere it cracks ; and so the skipper's lip was trem-
    bling for an oath

At the watch on deck for idleness, the watch below
    for sloth,

For the leash of his anathemas was long enough for
    both.

Well, 'twas burning noon off Java: Beans and
    Lambert in the chains
Sank their heads, and all was silent but the voices
    of their pains.
Night came ere their bonds were loosened; then
    the boys sank down and slept,
And the dew in place of loved ones on their
    wounded bodies wept.

All was still within the whaler, — on the sea no
    fanning breeze,
And the moon alone was moving over Java's gloomy
    trees.
Midnight came, — one sleeper's waking glance went
    out the moon to meet:
Nathan rose, and turned from Lambert, who still
    slumbered at his feet.
Out toward Java went his vision, as if something
    in the air
Came with promises of kindness and of peace to
    be found there.

Then towards the davits moved he, where the
    lightest whale-boat hung;
And he worked with silent caution till upon the
    sea she swung,
When he paused, and looked at Lambert, and the
    spirit in him cried
Not to leave him, but to venture, as since child-
    hood, side by side;
And the spirit's cry was answered, for he touched
    the sleeper's lip,
Who awoke and heard of Nathan's plan to leave
    th' accursed ship.

When 'twas told, they rose in silence, and looked
    outward to the land,
But they only saw Nantucket, with its homely,
    boat-lined strand;
But they saw it — oh! so plainly — through the
    glass of coming doom.
Then they crept into the whale-boat, and pulled
    toward the forest's gloom, —
All their suffering clear that moment, like the
    moonlight on their wake,

Now contracting, now expanding, like a phospho-
    rescent snake.

Hours speed on: the dark horizon yet shows scarce
    a streak of gray

When old Sculpin comes on deck to walk his rest-
    lessness away.

All the scene is still and solemn, and mayhap the
    man's cold heart

Feels its teaching, for the wild-beast cries from
    shoreward make him start

As if they had warning in them, and he o'er its
    meaning pored,

Till at length one shriek from Java splits the dark-
    ness like a sword;

And he almost screams in answer, such the nearness
    of the cry,

As he clutches at the rigging with a horror in his
    eye,

And with faltering accents mutters, as against the
    mast he leans,

" *Darn the tigers! that one shouted with the voice of
    Nathan Beans!* "

When the boys were missed soon after, Sculpin
    never breathed a word
Of his terror in the morning at the fearful sound
    he 'd heard ;
But he entered in the log-book, and 'twas witnessed
    by the mates,
Just their names, and following after, " Ran away
    in Sunda Straits."

Two years after, Captain Sculpin saw again the
    Yankee shore,
With the comfortable feeling that he 'd go to sea no
    more.
And 'twas strange the way he altered when he saw
    Nantucket light :
Holy lines spread o'er his face, and chased the old
    ones out of sight.
And for many a year thereafter did his zeal spread
    far and wide,
And with all his pious doings was the township
    edified ;

For he led the sacred singing in an unctuous, nasal
    tone,
And he looked as if the sermon and the Scriptures
    were his own.

But one day the white-haired preacher spoke of
    how God's justice fell
Soon or late with awful sureness on the man whose
    heart could tell
Of a wrong done to the widow or the orphan, and
    he said
That such wrongs were ever living, though the
    injured ones were dead.
And old Sculpin's heart was writhing, though his
    heavy eyes were closed, —
For, despite his solemn sanctity, at sermon times he
    dozed ;
But his half-awakened senses heard the preacher
    speak of death
And of wrongs done unto orphans, and he dreamed
    with wheezing breath

That old hands were tearing from his heart its
    pharisaic screens,
That the preacher was a tiger with the voice of
    Nathan Beans!
And he shrieked and jumped up wildly, and upon
    the seat stood he,
As if standing on the whaler looking outward on
    the sea;
And he clutched as at the rigging with a horror in
    his eye,
For he saw the woods of Java and he heard that
    human cry,
As he crouched and cowered earthward. And the
    simple folk around
Stood with looks of kindly sympathy: they raised
    him from the ground,
And they brought him half unconscious to the hum-
    ble chapel door,
Whence he fled as from a scourging, and he entered
    it no more;
For the sight of that old preacher brought the
    horror to his face,

And he dare not meet his neighbors' honest eyes
    within the place,
For his conscience like a mirror rose and showed
    the dismal scenes,
Where the tiger yelled for ever with the voice of
    Nathan Beans.

WESTERN AUSTRALIA.

Nation of sun and sin,
Thy flowers and crimes are red,
And thy heart is sore within
While the glory crowns thy head.
Land of the songless birds,
What was thine ancient crime,
Burning through lapse of time
Like a prophet's cursing words ?

Aloes and myrrh and tears
Mix in thy bitter wine :
Drink, while the cup is thine,
Drink, for the draught is sign
Of thy reign in the coming years.

PROLOGUE.

Nor gold nor silver are the words set here,
  Nor rich-wrought chasing on design of art;
But rugged relics of an unknown sphere
  Where fortune chanced I played one time a part.
Unthought of here the critic blame or praise,
  These recollections all their faults atone;
To hold the scenes, I've writ of men and ways
  Uncouth and rough as Austral ironstone.

It may be, I have left the higher gleams
  Of skies and flowers unheeded or forgot;
It may be so, — but, looking back, it seems
  When I was with them I beheld them not.
I was no rambling poet, but a man
  Hard-pressed to dig and delve, with naught of ease
The hot day through, save when the evening's fan
  Of sea-winds rustled through the kindly trees.

It may be so; but when I think I smile
  At my poor hand and brain to paint the charms
Of God's first-blazoned canvas! here the aisle
  Moonlit and deep of reaching gothic arms

From towering gum, mahogany, and palm,
  And odorous jam and sandal; there the growth
Of arm-long velvet leaves grown hoar in calm, —
  In calm unbroken since their luscious·youth.

How can I show you all the silent birds
  With strange metallic glintings on the wing?
Or how tell half their sadness in cold words, —
  The poor dumb lutes, the birds that never sing?
Of wondrous parrot-greens and iris hue
  Of sensuous flower and of gleaming snake, —
Ah! what I see I long that so might you,
  But of these things what picture can I make?

Sometime, maybe, a man will wander there, —
  A mind God-gifted, and not dull and weak;
And he will come and paint that land so fair,
  And show the beauties of which I but speak.
But in the hard, sad days that there I spent,
  My mind absorbed rude pictures: these I show
As best I may, and just with this intent, —
  To tell some things that all folk may not know.

WESTERN AUSTRALIA.

O BEAUTEOUS Southland! land of yellow
    air,
  That hangeth o'er thee slumbering, and doth hold
The moveless foliage of thy valleys fair
  And wooded hills, like aureole of gold.

O thou, discovered ere the fitting time,
  Ere Nature in completion turned thee forth!
Ere aught was finished but thy peerless clime,
  Thy virgin breath allured the amorous North.

O land, God made thee wondrous to the eye!
  But His sweet singers thou hast never heard;
He left thee, meaning to come by-and-bye,
  And give rich voice to every bright-winged bird.

He painted with fresh hues thy myriad flowers,
    But left them scentless: ah! their woful dole,
Like sad reproach of their Creator's powers, —
    To make so sweet fair bodies, void of soul.

He gave thee trees of odorous precious wood ;
    But, midst them all, bloomed not one tree of fruit.
He looked, but said not that His work was good,
    When leaving thee all perfumeless and mute.

He blessed thy flowers with honey: every bell
    Looks earthward, sunward, with a yearning wist;
But no bee-lover ever notes the swell
    Of hearts, like lips, a-hungering to be kist.

O strange land, thou art virgin! thou art more
    Than fig-tree barren!   Would that I could paint
For others' eyes the glory of the shore
    Where last I saw thee; but the senses faint

In soft delicious dreaming when they drain
    Thy wine of color.   Virgin fair thou art,
All sweetly fruitful, waiting with soft pain
    The spouse who comes to wake thy sleeping
    heart.

THE DUKITE SNAKE:

A WEST AUSTRALIAN BUSHMAN'S STORY.

WELL, mate, you 've asked me about a fellow
You met to-day, in a black-and-yellow
Chain-gang suit, with a pedler's pack,
Or with some such burden, strapped to his back.
Did you meet him square? No, passed you by?
Well, if you had, and had looked in his eye,
You 'd have felt for your irons then and there;
For the light in his eye is a madman's glare.
Ay, mad, poor fellow! I know him well,
And if you 're not sleepy just yet, I 'll tell
His story, — a strange one as ever you heard
Or read; but I 'll vouch for it, every word.

You just wait a minute, mate: I must see
How that damper 's doing, and make some tea.

You smoke? That's good; for there's plenty of
　　weed
In that wallaby skin. Does your horse feed
In the hobbles? Well, he's got good feed here,
And my own old bushmare won't interfere.
Done with that meat? Throw it there to the
　　dogs,
And fling on a couple of banksia logs.

And now for the story. That man who goes
Through the bush with the pack and the convict's
　　clothes
Has been mad for years; but he does no harm,
And our lonely settlers feel no alarm
When they see or meet him. Poor Dave Sloane
Was a settler once, and a friend of my own.
Some eight years back, in the spring of the year,
Dave came from Scotland, and settled here.
A splendid young fellow he was just then,
And one of the bravest and truest men
That I ever met: he was kind as a woman
To all who needed a friend, and no man —

Not even a convict — met with his scorn,
For David Sloane was a gentleman born.
Ay, friend, a gentleman, though it sounds queer :
There's plenty of blue blood flowing out here,
And some younger sons of your "upper ten"
Can be met with here, first-rate bushmen.
Why, friend, *I*—

            Bah! curse that dog!   you see
This talking so much has affected me.

Well, Sloane came here with an axe and a gun;
He bought four miles of a sandal-wood run.
This bush at that time was a lonesome place,
So lonesome the sight of a white man's face
Was a blessing, unless it came at night,
And peered in your hut, with the cunning fright
Of a runaway convict; and even they
Were welcome, for talk's sake, while they could
      stay.
Dave lived with me here for a while, and learned
The tricks of the bush, — how the snare was laid
In the wallaby track, how traps were made,

How 'possums and kangaroo rats were killed,
And when that was learned, I helped him to build
From mahogany slabs a good bush hut,
And showed him how sandal-wood logs were cut.
I lived up there with him days and days,
For I loved the lad for his honest ways.
I had only one fault to find: at first
Dave worked too hard; for a lad who was nursed,
As he was, in idleness, it was strange
How he cleared that sandal-wood off his range.
From the morning light till the light expired
He was always working, he never tired;
Till at length I began to think his will
Was too much settled on wealth, and still
When I looked at the lad's brown face, and eye
Clear open, my heart gave such thought the lie.
But one day — for he read my mind — he laid
His hand on my shoulder: " Don't be afraid,"
Said he, " that I 'm seeking alone for pelf.
I work hard, friend; but 'tis not for myself."

And he told me then, in his quiet tone,
Of a girl in Scotland, who was his own, —

His wife, — 'twas for her: 'twas all he could say,
And his clear eye brimmed as he turned away.
After that he told me the simple tale:
They had married for love, and she was to sail
For Australia when he wrote home and told
The oft-watched-for story of finding goid.

In a year he wrote, and his news was good:
He had bought some cattle and sold his wood.
He said, " Darling, I 've only a hut, — but come."
Friend, a husband's heart is a true wife's home;
And he knew she 'd come. Then he turned his hand
To make neat the house, and prepare the land
For his crops and vines; and he made that place
Put on such a smiling and homelike face,
That when she came, and he showed her round
His sandal-wood and his crops in the ground,
And spoke of the future, they cried for joy,
The husband's arm clasping his wife and boy.

Well, friend, if a little of heaven's best bliss
Ever comes from the upper world to this,

It came into that manly bushman's life,
And circled him round with the arms of his **wife.**
God bless that bright memory! Even to me,
A rough, lonely man, did she seem to be,
While living, an angel of God's pure love,
And now I could pray to her face above.
And David he loved her as only a man
With a heart as large as was his heart **can.**
I wondered how they could have lived **apart,**
For he was her idol, and she his heart.

Friend, there isn't much more of the tale to **tell:**
I was talking of angels awhile since. Well,
Now I'll change to a devil, — ay, to a devil!
You need n't start: if a spirit of evil
Ever came to this world its hate to slake
On mankind, it came as a Dukite Snake.

Like? Like the pictures you 've seen of Sin,
A long red snake, — as if what was within
Was fire that gleamed through his glistening
    skin.

And his eyes! — if you could go down to hell
And come back to your fellows here and tell
What the fire was like, you could find no thing,
Here below on the earth, or up in the sky,
To compare it to but a Dukite's eye!

Now, mark you, these Dukites don't go alone:
There 's another near when you see but one;
And beware you of killing that one you see
Without finding the other; for you may be
More than twenty miles from the spot that night,
When camped, but you 're tracked by the lone
　　Dukite,
That will follow your trail like Death or Fate,
And kill you as sure as you killed its mate!

Well, poor Dave Sloane had his young wife here
Three months, — 'twas just this time of the year.
He had teamed some sandal-wood to the Vasse,
And was homeward bound, when he saw in the
　　grass
A long red snake: he had never been told

Of the Dukite's ways, — he jumped to the road,
And smashed its flat head with the bullock-goad!

He was proud of the red skin, so he tied
Its tail to the cart, and the snake's blood dyed
The bush on the path he followed that night.

He was early home, and the dead Dukite
Was flung at the door to be skinned next **day.**
At sunrise next morning he started away
To hunt up his cattle.   A three hours' ride
Brought him back: he gazed on his home with pride
And joy in his heart; he jumped from his horse
And entered — to look on his young wife's corse,
And his dead child clutching its mother's clothes
As in fright; and there, as he gazed, arose
From her breast, where 'twas resting, the gleaming
    head
Of the terrible Dukite, as if it said,
"*I've had vengeance, my foe: you took all I had.*"

And so had the snake — David Sloane was mad!

I rode to his hut just by chance that night,
And there on the threshold the clear moonlight
Showed the two snakes dead. I pushed in the
    door
With an awful feeling of coming woe :
The dead were stretched on the moonlit floor,
The man held the hand of his wife, — his pride,
His poor life's treasure, — and crouched by her
    side.
O God! I sank with the weight of the blow.
I touched and called him : he heeded me not,
So I dug her grave in a quiet spot,
And lifted them both, — her boy on her breast, —
And laid them down in the shade to rest.
Then I tried to take my poor friend away,
But he cried so wofully, " Let me stay
Till she comes again ! " that I had no heart
To try to persuade him then to part
From all that was left to him here, — her grave ;
So I stayed by his side that night, and, save
One heart-cutting cry, he uttered no sound, —
O God! that wail — like the wail of a hound!

'Tis six long years since I heard that cry,
But 'twill ring in my ears till the day I die.
Since that fearful night no one has heard
Poor David Sloane utter sound or word.
You have seen to-day how he always goes:
He's been given that suit of convict's clothes
By some prison officer. On his back
You noticed a load like a pedler's pack?
Well, that's what he lives for: when reason went,
Still memory lived, for his days are spent
In searching for Dukites; and year by year
That bundle of skins is growing. 'Tis clear
That the Lord out of evil some good still takes;
For he's clearing this bush of the Dukite snakes.

THE MONSTER DIAMOND:

A TALE OF THE PENAL COLONY OF WEST AUSTRALIA

"I 'LL have it, I tell you! Curse you!—there!"
   The long knife glittered, was sheathed, and
   was bare.
The sawyer staggered and tripped and fell,
And falling he uttered a frightened yell:
His face to the sky, he shuddered and gasped,
And tried to put from him the man he had grasped
A moment before in the terrible strife.
"I 'll have it, I tell you, or have your life!
Where is it?" The sawyer grew weak, but still
His brown face gleamed with a desperate will.
"Where is it?" he heard, and the red knife's drip
In his slayer's hand fell down on his lip.
"Will you give it?" "Never!" A curse, the knife
Was raised and buried.

Thus closed the life
Of Samuel Jones, known as " Number **Ten** "
On his Ticket-of-Leave ; and of all the **men**
In the Western Colony, bond or free,
None had manlier heart or hand than **he.**

In digging a sawpit, while all alone, —
For his mate was sleeping, — Sam struck a stone
With the edge of the spade, and it gleamed like
      fire,
And looked at Sam from its bed in the mire,
Till he dropped the spade and stooped and raised
The wonderful stone that glittered and blazed
As if it were mad at the spade's rude blow ;
But its blaze set the sawyer's heart aglow
As he looked and trembled, then turned him round,
And crept from the pit, and lay on the ground,
Looking over the mould-heap at the camp
Where his mate still slept. Then down to the
      swamp
He ran with the stone, and washed it bright,
And felt like a drunken man at the sight

Of a diamond pure as spring-water and sun,
And larger than ever man's eyes looked on!

Then down sat Sam with the stone on his knees,
And fancies came to him, like swarms of bees
To a sugar-creamed hive; and he dreamed awake
Of the carriage and four in which he'd take
His pals from the Dials to Drury Lane,
The silks and the satins for Susan Jane,
The countless bottles of brandy and beer
He'd call for and pay for, and every year
The dinner he'd give to the Brummagem lads, —
He'd be king among cracksmen and chief among
      pads,
And he'd sport a —

                    Over him stooped his mate,
A pick in his hand, and his face all hate.
Sam saw the shadow, and guessed the pick,
And closed his dream with a spring so quick
The purpose was baffled of Aaron Mace,
And the sawyer mates stood face to face.

Sam folded his arms across his chest,
Having thrust the stone in his loose shirt-breast,
While he tried to think where he dropped the spade.
But Aaron Mace wore a long, keen blade
In his belt, — he drew it. — sprang on his man:
What happened, you read when the tale began.

Then he looked — the murderer, Aaron Mace —
At the gray-blue lines in the dead man's face;
And he turned away, for he feared its frown
More in death than life. Then he knelt him down, —
Not to pray, — but he shrank from the staring eyes,
And felt in the breast for the fatal prize.
And this was the man, and this was the way
That he took the stone on its natal day;
And for this he was cursed for evermore
By the West Australian Koh-i-nor.

In the half-dug pit the corpse was thrown,
And the murderer stood in the camp alone.
Alone? No, no! never more was he
To part from the terrible company

Of that gray-blue face and the bleeding breast
And the staring eyes in their awful rest.
The evening closed on the homicide,
And the blood of the buried sawyer cried
Through the night to God, and the shadows dark
That crossed the camp had the stiff and stark
And horrible look of a murdered man!
Then he piled the fire, and crept within
The ring of its light, that closed him in
Like tender mercy, and drove away
For a time the spectres that stood at bay,
And waited to clutch him as demons wait,
Shut out from the sinner by Faith's bright gate.
But the fire burnt low, and the slayer slept,
And the key of his sleep was always kept
By the leaden hand of him he had slain,
That oped the door but to drench the brain
With agony cruel.   The night wind crept
Like a snake on the shuddering form that slept
And dreamt, and woke and shrieked; for there,
With its gray-blue lines and its ghastly stare,

Cutting into the vitals of Aaron Mace,
In the flickering light was the sawyer's face!

Evermore 'twas with him, that dismal sight, —
The white face set in the frame of night.
He wandered away from the spot, but found
No inch of the West Australian ground
Where he could hide from the bleeding breast,
Or sink his head in a dreamless rest.

And always with him he bore the prize
In a pouch of leather: the staring eyes
Might burn his soul, but the diamond's gleam
Was solace and joy for the haunted dream.

So the years rolled on, while the murderer's mind
Was bent on a futile quest, — to find
A way of escape from the blood-stained soil
And the terrible wear of the penal toil.

But this was a part of the diamond's curse, —
The toil that was heavy before grew worse,

Till the panting wretch in his fierce unrest
Would clutch the pouch as it lay on his breast,
And waking cower, with sob and moan,
Or shriek wild curses against the stone
That was only a stone ; for he could not sell,
And he dare not break, and he feared to tell
Of his wealth: so he bore it through hopes and
    fears —
His God and his devil — for years and years.

And thus did he draw near the end of his race,
With a form bent double and horror-lined face,
And a piteous look, as if asking for grace
Or for kindness from some one ; but no kind word
Was flung to his misery: shunned, abhorred,
E'en by wretches themselves, till his life was a
    curse,
And he thought that e'en death could bring nothing
    worse
Than the phantoms that stirred at the diamond's
    weight, —
His own life's ghost and the ghost of his mate.

So he turned one day from the haunts of men,
And their friendless faces: an old man then,
In a convict's garb, with white flowing hair,
And a brow deep seared with the word, "Despair."
He gazed not back as his way he took
To the untrod forest; and oh! the look,
The piteous look in his sunken eyes,
Told that life was the bitterest sacrifice.

But little was heard of his later days:
'Twas deemed in the West that in change of **ways**
He tried with his tears to wash out the sin.
'Twas told by some natives who once came in
From the Kojunup Hills, that lonely there
They had seen a figure with long white hair;
They encamped close by where his hut was made,
And were scared at night when they saw he prayed
To the white man's God; and on one wild night
They had heard his voice till the morning light.

Years passed, and a sandalwood-cutter stood
At a ruined hut in a Kojunup wood:

The rank weeds covered the desolate floor,
And an ant-hill stood on the fallen door;
The cupboard within to the snakes was loot,
And the hearth was the home of the bandicoot.
But neither at hut nor snake nor rat
Was the woodcutter staring intent, but at
A human skeleton clad in gray,
The hands clasped over the breast, as they
Had fallen in peace when he ceased to pray.

As the bushman looked on the form, he saw
In the breast a paper: he stooped to draw
What might tell him the story, but at his touch
From under the hands rolled a leathern pouch,
And he raised it too, — on the paper's face
He read " Ticket-of-Leave of Aaron Mace."
Then he opened the pouch, and in dazed surprise
At its contents strange he unblessed his eyes:
'Twas a lump of quartz, — a pound weight in full, —
And it fell from his hand on the skeleton's skull!

THE DOG GUARD: AN AUSTRALIAN STORY.

THERE are lonesome places upon the earth
　　That have never re-echoed a sound of mirth,
Where the spirits abide that feast and quaff
On the shuddering soul of a murdered laugh,
And take grim delight in the fearful start,
As their unseen fingers clutch the heart,
And the blood flies out from the griping pain,
To carry the chill through every vein;
And the staring eyes and the whitened faces
Are a joy to these ghosts of the lonesome places.

But of all the spots on this earthly sphere
Where these dismal spirits are strong and near,
There is one more dreary than all the rest, —
'Tis the barren island of Rottenest.
On Australia's western coast, you may —
On a seaman's chart of Fremantle Bay —

Find a tiny speck, some ten miles from shore :
If the chart be good, there is something more, —
For a shoal runs in on the landward side,
With five fathoms marked for the highest tide.
You have nought but my word for all the rest,
But that speck is the island of Rottenest.

'Tis a white sand-heap, about two miles long,
And say half as wide ; but the deeds of wrong
Between man and his brother that there took place
Are sufficient to sully a continent's face.
Ah, cruel tales ! were they told as a whole,
They would scare your polished humanity's soul ;
They would blanch the cheeks in your carpeted
    room,
With a terrible thought of the merited doom
For the crimes committed, still unredrest,
On that white sand-heap called Rottenest.

Of late years the island is not so bare
As it was when I saw it first; for there
On the outer headland some buildings stand,

And a flag, red-crossed, says the patch of sand
Is a recognized part of the wide domain
That is blessed with the peace of Victoria's reign.
But behind the lighthouse the land 's the same,
And it bears grim proof of the white man's shame;
For the miniature vales that the island owns
Have a horrible harvest of human bones!

And how did they come there? that 's the word;
And I 'll answer it now with the tale I heard
From the lips of a man who was there, and saw
The bad end of man's greed and of colony law.

Many years ago, when the white man first
Set his foot on the coast, and was hated and cursed
By the native, who had not yet learned to fear
The dark wrath of the stranger, but drove his spear
With a freeman's force and a bushman's yell
At the white invader, it then befell
That so many were killed and cooked and eaten,
There was risk of the whites in the end being
    beaten;

So a plan was proposed, — 'twas deemed safest and
    best
To imprison the natives in Rottenest.

And so every time there was white blood spilled,
There were black men captured; and those not
    killed
In the rage of vengeance were sent away
To this bleak sand isle in Fremantle Bay;
And it soon came round that a thousand men
Were together there, like wild beasts in a pen.
There was not a shrub or grass-blade in the sand,
Nor a piece of timber as large as your hand;
But a government boat went out each day
To fling meat ashore — and then sailed away.

For a year or so was this course pursued,
Till 'twas noticed that fewer came down for food
When the boat appeared; then a guard lay round
The island one night, and the white men found
That the savages swam at the lowest tide
To the shoal that lay on the landward side, —

'Twas a mile from the beach, — and then waded
    ashore ;
So the settlers met in grave council once more.

That a guard was needed was plain to all ;
But nobody answered the Governor's call
For a volunteer watch.   They were only a few,
And their wild young farms gave plenty to do ;
And the council of settlers was breaking up,
With a dread of the sorrow they 'd have to sup
When the savage, unawed, and for vengeance wild.
Lay await in the wood for the mother and child.
And with doleful countenance each to his neighbor
Told a dreary tale of the world of labor
He had, and said, " Let him watch who can,
I can't ; " when there stepped to the front a
    man
With a hard brown face and a burglar's brow,
Who had learned the secret he uttered now
When he served in the chain-gang in New South
    Wales.
And he said to them : " Friends, as all else fails,

These 'ere natives are safe as if locked and barred,
If you 'll line that shoal with a mastiff guard!"

And the settlers looked at each other awhile,
Till the wonder toned to a well-pleased smile
When the brown ex-burglar said he knew,
And would show the whole of 'em what to do.

Some three weeks after, the guard was set;
And a native who swam to the shoal was met
By two half-starved dogs, when a mile from
    shore, —
And, somehow, that native was never seen more.
All the settlers were pleased with the capital plan,
And they voted their thanks to the hard-faced
    man.
For a year, each day did the government boat
Take the meat to the isle and its guard afloat.
In a line, on the face of the shoal, the dogs
Had a dry house each, on some anchored logs;
And the neck-chain from each stretched just half
    way

To the next dog's house; right across the Bay
Ran a line that was hideous with horrid sounds
From the hungry throats of two hundred hounds.

So one more year passed, and the brutes on the logs
Had grown more like devils than common dogs.
There was such a hell-chorus by day and night
That the settlers ashore were chilled with fright
When they thought — if that legion should break
    away,
And come in with the tide some fatal day!

But they 'scaped that chance; for a man came in
From the Bush, one day, with a 'possum's skin
To the throat filled up with large pearls he 'd found
To the north, on the shore of the Shark's Bay
    Sound.
And the settlement blazed with a wild commotion
At sight of the gems from the wealthy ocean.

Then the settlers all began to pack
Their tools and tents, and to ask the track

That the bushman followed to strike the spot, —
While the dogs and natives were all forgot.
In two days, from that camp on the River Swan,
To the Shark's Bay Sound had the settlers gone ;
And no merciful feeling did one retard
For the helpless men and their terrible guard.

It were vain to try, in my quiet room,
To write down the truth of the awful doom
That befell those savages prisoned there,
When the pangs of hunger and wild despair
Had nigh made them mad as the fiends outside :
'Tis enough that one night, through the low ebb
    tide,
Swam nine hundred savages, armed with stones
And with weapons made from their dead friends'
    bones.
Without ripple or sound, when the moon was gone,
Through the inky water they glided on ;
Swimming deep, and scarce daring to draw a breath,
While the guards, if they saw, were as dumb as
    death.

'Twas a terrible picture! O God! that the night
Were so black as to cover the horrid sight
From the eyes of the Angel that notes man s ways
In the book that will ope on the Day of Days!

There were screams when they met, — shrill screams
    of pain!
For each animal swam at the length of his chain,
And with parching throat and in furious mood
Lay awaiting, not men, but his coming food.
There were short, sharp cries, and a line of fleck
As the long fangs sank in the swimmer's neck;
There were gurgling growls mixed with human
    groans,
For the savages drave the sharpened bones
Through their enemies' ribs, and the bodies sank,
Each dog holding fast with a bone through his flank,

Then those of the natives who 'scaped swam back;
But too late! for scores of the savage pack,
Driven mad by the yells and the sounds of fight,
Had broke loose and followed. On that dread night

Let the curtain fall: when the red sun rose
From the placid ocean, the joys and woes
Of a thousand men he had last eve seen
Were as things or thoughts that had never been.

When the settlers returned, — in a month or two, —
They bethought of the dogs and the prisoned crew.
And a boat went out on a tardy quest
Of whatever was living on Rottenest.
They searched all the isle, and sailed back agen
With some specimen bones of the dogs and men.

THE AMBER WHALE.

Though it lash the shallows that line the beach,
    Afar from the great sea deeps,
There is never a storm whose might can reach
    Where the vast leviathan sleeps.
Like a mighty thought in a quiet mind,
    In the clear, cold depths he swims ;
Whilst above him the pettiest form of his kind
    With a dash o'er the surface skims.

There is peace in power : the men who speak
    With the loudest tongues do least ;
And the surest sign of a mind that is weak
    Is its want of the power to rest.
It is only the lighter water that flies
    From the sea on a windy day ;
And the deep blue ocean never replies
    To the sibilant voice of the spray.

THE AMBER WHALE: A HARPOONEER'S STORY.

[Whalemen have a strange belief as to the formation of amber. They say that it is a petrifaction of some internal part of a whale; and they tell weird stories of enormous whales seen in the warm latitudes, that were almost entirely transformed into the precious substance.]

WE were down in the Indian Ocean, after
    sperm, and three years out;
The last six months in the tropics, and looking
    in vain for a spout,—
Five men up on the royal yards, weary of strain-
    ing their sight;
And every day like its brother,—just morning and
    noon and night—
Nothing to break the sameness: water and wind
    and sun
Motionless, gentle, and blazing,—never a change
    in one.

Every day like its brother: when the noonday
    eight-bells came,
'Twas like yesterday; and we seemed to know
    that to-morrow would be the same.
The foremast hands had a lazy time: there was
    never a thing to do;
The ship was painted, tarred down, and scraped;
    and the mates had nothing new.
We'd worked at sinnet and ratline till there wasn't
    a yarn to use,
And all we could do was watch and pray for a
    sperm whale's spout — or news.
It was whaler's luck of the vilest sort; and, though
    many a volunteer
Spent his watch below on the look-out, never a
    whale came near, —
At least of the kind we wanted: there were lots
    of whales of a sort, —
Killers and finbacks, and such like, as if they
    enjoyed the sport
Of seeing a whale-ship idle; but we never lowered
    a boat

For less than a blackfish, — there's no oil in a
killer's or finback's coat.
There was rich reward for the look-out men, —
tobacco for even a sail,
And a barrel of oil for the lucky dog who 'd be
first to " raise " a whale.
The crew was a mixture from every land, and many
a tongue they spoke ;
And when they sat in the fo'castle, enjoying an
evening smoke,
There were tales told, youngster, would make you
stare, — stories of countless shoals
Of devil-fish in the Pacific and right-whales away
at the Poles.
There was one of these fo'castle yarns that we
always loved to hear, —
Kanaka and Maori and Yankee ; all lent an eager
ear
To that strange old tale that was always new, —
the wonderful treasure-tale
Of an old Down-Eastern harpooneer who had
struck an Amber Whale !

Ay, that was a tale worth hearing, lad: if 'twas
    true we couldn't say,
Or if 'twas a yarn old Mat had spun to while the
    time away.

"It 's just fifteen years ago," said Mat, "since I
    shipped as harpooneer
On board a bark in New Bedford, and came cruis-
    ing somewhere near
To this whaling-ground we 're cruising now; but
    whales were plenty then,
And not like now, when we scarce get oil to pay
    for the ship and men.
There were none of these oil wells running then, —
    at least, what shore folk term
An oil well in Pennsylvania, — but sulphur-bottom
    and sperm
Were plenty as frogs in a mud-hole, and all of 'em
    big whales, too ;
One hundred barrels for sperm-whales; and for
    sulphur-bottom, two.
You couldn't pick out a small one: the littlest
    calf or cow

Had a sight more oil than the big bull whales we
    think so much of now.

We were more to the east, off Java Straits, a little
    below the mouth, —

A hundred and five to the east'ard and nine de-
    grees to the south;

And that was as good a whaling-ground for mid-
    dling-sized, handy whales

As any in all the ocean; and 'twas always white
    with sails

From Scotland and Hull and New England, — for
    the whales were thick as frogs,

And 'twas little trouble to kill 'em then, for they
    lay as quiet as logs.

And every night we 'd go visiting the other whale-
    ships 'round,

Or p'r'aps we 'd strike on a Dutchman, calmed off
    the Straits, and bound

To Singapore or Batavia, with plenty of schnapps
    to sell

For a few whale's teeth or a gallon of oil, and the
    latest news to tell.

And in every ship of that whaling fleet was one
    wonderful story told, —
How an Amber Whale had been seen that year
    that was worth a mint of gold.
And one man — mate of a Scotchman — said he 'd
    seen, away to the west,
A big school of sperm, and one whale's spout was
    twice as high as the rest;
And we knew that that was the Amber Whale, for
    we 'd often heard before
That his spout was twice as thick as the rest, and
    a hundred feet high or more.
And often, when the look-out cried, ' He blows!'
    the very hail
Thrilled every heart with the greed of gold, — for
    we thought of the Amber Whale.

" But never a sight of his spout we saw till the sea-
    son there went round,
And the ships ran down to the south'ard to an-
    other whaling-ground.

We stayed to the last off Java, and then we ran
    to the west,

To get our recruits at Mauritius, and give the crew
    a rest.

Five days we ran in the trade winds, and the boys
    were beginning to talk

Of their time ashore, and whether they 'd have a
    donkey-ride or a walk,

And whether they 'd spend their money in wine,
    bananas, or pearls,

Or drive to the sugar plantations to dance with the
    Creole girls.

But they soon got something to talk about. Five
    days we ran west-sou'-west,

But the sixth day's log-book entry was a change
    from all the rest ;

For that was the day the mast-head men made
    every face turn pale,

With the cry that we all had dreamt about, — ' HE
    BLOWS ! THE AMBER WHALE ! '

" And every man was motionless, and every speak-
  er's lip
Just stopped as it was, with the word half-said:
  there wasn't a sound in the ship
Till the Captain hailed the masthead, ' Whereaway
  is the whale you see ? '
And the cry came down again, ' He blows! about
  four points on our lee,
And three miles off, sir, — there he blows! he 's
  going to leeward fast! '
And then we sprang to the rigging, and saw the
  great whale at last!

" Ah! shipmates, that was a sight to see: the water
  was smooth as a lake,
And there was the monster rolling, with a school of
  whales in his wake.
They looked like pilot-fish round a shark, as if they
  were keeping guard;
And, shipmates, the spout of that Amber Whale
  was high as a sky-sail yard.
There was never a ship's crew worked so quick as
  our whalemen worked that day, —

When the captain shouted, 'Swing the boats, and
    be ready to lower away!'
Then, 'A pull on the weather-braces, men! let her
    head fall off three points!'
And off she swung, with a quarter-breeze straining
    the old ship's joints.
The men came down from the mastheads; and the
    boats' crews stood on the rail,
Stowing the lines and irons, and fixing paddles and
    sail.
And when all was ready we leant on the boats and
    looked at the Amber's spout,
That went up like a monster fountain, with a sort
    of a rumbling shout,
Like a thousand railroad engines puffing away their
    smoke.
He was just like a frigate's hull capsized, and the
    swaying water broke
Against the sides of the great stiff whale: he was
    steering south-by-west, —
For the Cape, no doubt, for a whale can shape a
    course as well as the best.

We soon got close as was right to go ; for the school
    might hear a hail,
Or see the bark, and that was the last of our Bank-
    of-England Whale.
'Let her luff,' said the Old Man, gently. 'Now,
    lower away, my boys,
And pull for a mile, then paddle, — and mind that
    you make no noise.'

"A minute more, and the boats were down; and
    out from the hull of the bark
They shot with a nervous sweep of the oars, like
    dolphins away from a shark.
Each officer stood in the stern, and watched, as he
    held the steering oar,
And the crews bent down to their pulling as they
    never pulled before.

" Our Mate was as thorough a whaleman as I ever
    met afloat ;
And I was his harpooneer that day, and sat in the
    bow of the boat.

His eyes were set on the whales ahead, and he spoke
    in a low, deep tone,
And told the men to be steady and cool, and the
    whale was all our own.
And steady and cool they proved to be : you could
    read it in every face,
And in every straining muscle, that they meant to
    win that race.
'Bend to it, boys, for a few strokes more, — bend to
    it steady and long !
Now, in with your oars, and paddles out, — all
    together, and strong !'
Then we turned and sat on the gunwale, with our
    faces to the bow ;
And the whales were right ahead, — no more than
    four ships' lengths off now.
There were five of 'em, hundred-barrellers, like
    guards round the Amber Whale.
And to strike him we 'd have to risk being stove by
    crossing a sweeping tail ;
But the prize and the risk were equal. 'Mat,' now
    whispers the Mate,

'Are your irons ready?' 'Ay, ay, sir.' 'Stand up,
   then, steady, and wait
Till I give the word, then let 'em fly, and hit him
   below the fin
As he rolls to wind'ard. Start her, boys! now's
   the time to slide her in!
Hurrah! that fluke just missed us. Mind, as soon
   as the iron's fast,
Be ready to back your paddles, — now in for it, boys,
   at last.
Heave! Again!'

     "And two irons flew: the first one sank
  in the joint,
'Tween the head and hump, — in the muscle; but
   the second had its point
Turned off by striking the amber case, coming out
   again like a bow,
And the monster carcass quivered, and rolled with
   pain from the first deep blow.
Then he lashed the sea with his terrible flukes, and
   showed us many a sign

That his rage was roused. 'Lay off,' roared the
    Mate, 'and all keep clear of the line!'
And that was a timely warning, for the whale made
    an awful breach
Right out of the sea; and 'twas well for us that the
    boat was beyond the reach
Of his sweeping flukes, as he milled around, and
    made for the Captain's boat,
That was right astern. And, shipmates, then my
    heart swelled up in my throat
At the sight I saw: the Amber Whale was lash-
    ing the sea with rage,
And two of his hundred-barrel guards were ready
    now to engage
In a bloody fight, and with open jaws they came
    to their master's aid.
Then we knew the Captain's boat was doomed; but
    the crew were no whit afraid, —
They were brave New England whalemen, — and
    we saw the harpooneer
Stand up to send in his irons, as soon as the whale
    came near.

Then we heard the Captain's order, ' Heave ! ' and
    saw the harpoon fly,
As the whales closed in with their open jaws : a
    shock, and a stifled cry
Was all that we heard ; then we looked to see if
    the crew were still afloat, —
But nothing was there save a dull red patch, and
    the boards of the shattered boat!

" But that was no time for mourning words : the
    other two boats came in,
And one got fast on the quarter, and one aft the
    starboard fin
Of the Amber Whale. For a minute he paused, as
    if he were in doubt
As to whether 'twas best to run or fight. ' Lay
    on ! ' the Mate roared out,
' And I 'll give him a lance ! ' The boat shot in ;
    and the Mate, when he saw his chance
Of sending it home to the vitals, four times he
    buried his lance.
A minute more, and a cheer went up, when we saw
    that his aim was good ;

For the lance had struck in a life-spot, and the whale
    was spouting blood!

But now came the time of danger, for the school of
    whales around

Had aired their flukes, and the cry was raised,
    'Look out! they're going to sound!'

And down they went with a sudden plunge, the
    Amber Whale the last,

While the lines ran smoking out of the tubs, he
    went to the deep so fast.

Before you could count your fingers, a hundred
    fathoms were out;

And then he stopped, for a wounded whale must
    come to the top and spout.

We hauled slack line as we felt him rise; and
    when he came up alone,

And spouted thick blood, we cheered again, for we
    knew he was all our own.

He was frightened now, and his fight was gone, —
    right round and round he spun,

As if he was trying to sight the boats, or find the
    best side to run.

But that was the minute for us to work: the boats
    hauled in their slack,

And bent on the drag-tubs over the stern to tire
    and hold him back.

The bark was five miles to wind'ard, and the mate
    gave a troubled glance

At the sinking sun, and muttered, ' Boys, we must
    give him another lance,

Or he 'll run till night; and, if he should head to
    wind'ard in the dark,

We 'll be forced to cut loose and leave him, or else
    lose run of the bark.'

So we hauled in close, two boats at once, but only
    frightened the whale;

And, like a hound that was badly whipped, he
    turned and showed his tail,

With his head right dead to wind'ard; then as
    straight and as swift he sped

As a hungry shark for a swimming prey; and,
    bending over his head,

Like a mighty plume, went his bloody spout. Ah!
    shipmates, that was a sight

Worth a life at sea to witness. In his wake the sea
  was white
As you 've seen it after a steamer's screw, churning
  up like foaming yeast ;
And the boats went hissing along at the rate of
  twenty knots at least.
With the water flush with the gunwale, and the
  oars were all apeak,
While the crews sat silent and quiet, watching the
  long, white streak
That was traced by the line of our passage. We
  hailed the bark as we passed,
And told them to keep a sharp look-out from the
  head of every mast ;
'And if we 're not back by sundown,' cried the
  Mate, 'you keep a light
At the royal cross-trees. If he dies, we may stick
  to the whale all night.'

"And past we swept with our oars apeak, and
  waved our hands to the hail
Of the wondering men on the taffrail, who were
  watching our Amber Whale

As he surged ahead, just as if he thought he could
    tire his enemies out;
I was almost sorrowful, shipmates, to see after each
    red spout
That the great whale's strength was failing: the
    sweep of his flukes grew slow,
Till at sundown he made about four knots, and his
    spout was weak and low.
Then said the Mate to his boat's crew: ' Boys, the
    vessel is out of sight
To the leeward: now, shall we cut the line, or stick
    to the whale all night?'
' We 'll stick to the whale!' cried every man. ' Let
    the other boats go back
To the vessel and beat to wind'ard, as well as they
    can, in our track.'
It was done as they said: the lines were cut, and
    the crews cried out, ' Good speed!'
As we swept along in the darkness, in the wake
    of our monster steed,
That went plunging on, with the dogged hope that
    he 'd tire his enemies still, —

But even the strength of an Amber Whale must
    break before human will.
By little and little his power had failed as he
    spouted his blood away,
Till at midnight the rising moon shone down on
    the great fish as he lay
Just moving his flukes; but at length he stopped,
    and raising his square, black head
As high as the topmast cross-trees, swung round
    and fell over — dead!

" And then rose a shout of triumph, — a shout that
    was more like a curse
Than an honest cheer; but, shipmates, the thought
    in our hearts was worse,
And 'twas punished with bitter suffering. We
    claimed the whale as our own,
And said that the crew should have no share of the
    wealth that was ours alone.
We said to each other: We want their help till we
    get the whale aboard,
So we 'll let 'em think that they 'll have a share till
    we get the Amber stored,

And then we 'll pay them their wages, and send
them ashore — *or afloat,*
If they show their temper. Ah! shipmates, no
wonder 'twas that boat
And its selfish crew were cursed that night. Next
day we saw no sail,
But the wind and sea were rising. Still, we held
to the drifting whale, —
And a dead whale drifts to windward, — going
farther away from the ship,
Without water, or bread, or courage to pray with
heart or lip
That had planned and spoken the treachery. The
wind blew into a gale,
And it screamed like mocking laughter round our
boat and the Amber Whale.

" That night fell dark on the starving crew, and a
hurricane blew next day;
Then we cut the line, and we cursed the prize as it
drifted fast away,
As if some power under the waves were towing it
out of sight;

And there we were, without help or hope, dreading
    the coming night.

Three days that hurricane lasted. When it passed,
    two men were dead ;

And the strongest one of the living had not strength
    to raise his head,

When his dreaming swoon was broken by the sound
    of a cheery hail,

And he saw a shadow fall on the boat, — it fell
    from the old bark's sail !

And when he heard their kindly words, you 'd think
    he should have smiled

With joy at his deliverance ; but he cried like a
    little child,

And hid his face in his poor weak hands, — for he
    thought of the selfish plan, —

And he prayed to God to forgive them all. And,
    shipmates, I am the man ! —

The only one of the sinful crew that ever beheld
    his home ;

For before the cruise was over, all the rest were
    under the foam.

It's just fifteen years gone, shipmates," said old
    Mat, ending his tale ;

" And I often pray that I 'll never see another
    Amber Whale."

THE KING OF THE VASSE.

A LEGEND OF THE BUSH.

From that fair land and drear land in the South,
  Of which through years I do not cease to think,
I brought a tale, learned not by word of mouth,
  But formed by finding here one golden link
And there another; and with hands unskilled
  For such fine work, but patient of all pain
For love of it, I sought therefrom to build
  What might have been at first the goodly chain.

It is not golden now: my craft knows more
  Of working baser metal than of fine;
but to those fate-wrought rings of precious ore
  I add these rugged iron links of mine.

THE KING OF THE VASSE.

A LEGEND OF THE BUSH.

MY tale which I have brought is of a time
    Ere that fair Southern land was stained with
    crime,
Brought thitherward in reeking ships and cast
Like blight upon the coast, or like a blast
From angry levin on a fair young tree,
That stands thenceforth a piteous sight to see.
So lives this land to-day beneath the sun,—
A weltering plague-spot, where the hot tears run,
And hearts to ashes turn, and souls are dried
Like empty kilns where hopes have parched and
    died.
Woe's cloak is round her,— she the fairest shore
In all the Southern Ocean o'er and o'er.
Poor Cinderella! she must bide her woe,
Because an elder sister wills it so.

Ah! could that sister see the future day
When her own wealth and strength are shorn
    away,
And she, lone mother then, puts forth her hand
To rest on kindred blood in that far land ;
Could she but see that kin deny her claim
Because of nothing owing her but shame, —
Then might she learn 'tis building but to fall,
If carted rubble be the basement-wall.

But this my tale, if tale it be, begins
Before the young land saw the old land's sins
Sail up the orient ocean, like a cloud
Far-blown, and widening as it neared, — a shroud
Fate-sent to wrap the bier of all things pure,
And mark the leper-land while stains endure.

In the far days, the few who sought the West
Were men all guileless, in adventurous quest
Of lands to feed their flocks and raise their grain,
And help them live their lives with less of pain
Than crowded Europe lets her children know.

From their old homesteads did they seaward go,
As if in Nature's order men must flee
As flow the streams, — from inlands to the sea.

In that far time, from out a Northern land,
With home-ties severed, went a numerous band
Of men and wives and children, white-haired
  folk:
Whose humble hope of rest at home had broke,
As year was piled on year, and still their toil
Had wrung poor fee from Sweden's rugged soil.
One day there gathered from the neighboring steads,
In Jacob Eibsen's, five strong household heads, —
Five men large-limbed and sinewed, Jacob's sons,
Though he was hale, as one whose current runs
In stony channels, that the streamlet rend,
But keep it clear and full unto the end.
Eight sons had Jacob Eibsen, — three still boys,
And these five men, who owned of griefs and
  joys
The common lot; and three tall girls beside,
Of whom the eldest was a blushing bride

One year before.   Old-fashioned times and men,
And wives and maidens, were in Sweden then.
These five came there for counsel: they were
    tired
Of hoping on for all the heart desired;
And Jacob, old but mighty-thewed as youth,
In all their words did sadly own the truth,
And said unto them, " Wealth cannot be found
In Sweden now by men who till the ground.
I 've thought at times of leaving this bare place,
And holding seaward with a seeking face
For those new lands they speak of, where men
    thrive.
Alone I 've thought of this; but now you five —
Five brother men of Eibsen blood — shall say
If our old stock from here must wend th ir
    way,
And seek a home where anxious sires can give
To every child enough whereon to live."

Then each took thought in silence.   Jacob gazed
Across them at the pastures worn and grazed

By ill-fed herds; his glance to corn-fields passed,
Where stunted oats, worse each year than the last,
And blighted barley, grew amongst the stones,
That showed ungainly, like earth's fleshless bones.
He sighed, and turned away. "Sons, let me know
What think you."

       Each one answered firm, "We go.'
And then they said, " We want no northern wind
To chill us more, or driving hail to blind.
But let us sail where south winds fan the sea,
And happier we and all our race shall be."
And so in time there started for the coast,
With farm and household gear, this Eibsen host;
And there, with others, to a good ship passed,
Which soon of Sweden's hills beheld the last.

I know not of their voyage, nor how they
Did wonder-stricken sit, as day by day,
'Neath tropic rays, they saw the smooth sea swell
And heave; while night by night the north-star
    fell,

Till last they watched him burning on the sea;
Nor how they saw, and wondered it could be,
Strange beacons rise before them as they gazed:
Nor how their hearts grew light when southward
    blazed
Five stars in blessed shape,—the Cross! whose
    flame
Seemed shining welcome as the wanderers came.

My story presses from this star-born hope
To where on young New Holland's western slope
These Northern farming folk found homes at
    last,
And all their thankless toil seemed now long
    past.

Nine fruitful years chased over, and nigh all
Of life was sweet.   But one dark drop of gall
Had come when first they landed, like a sign
Of some black woe; and deep in Eibsen's wine
Of life it hid, till in the sweetest cup
The old man saw its shape come shuddering up.

And first it came in this wise: when their ship
Had made the promised land, and every lip
Was pouring praise for what the eye did meet, —
For all the air was yellow as with heat
Above the peaceful sea and dazzling sand
That wooed each other round the beauteous land,
Where inward stretched the slumbering forest's
    green, —
When first these sights from off the deck were
    seen,
There rose a wailing sternwards, and the men
Who dreamt of heaven turned to earth agen,
And heard the direful cause with bated breath, —
The land's first gleam had brought the blight of
    death!

The wife of Eibsen held her six-years son,
Her youngest, and in secret best-loved one,
Close to her lifeless: his had been the cry
That first horizonwards bent every eye;
And from that opening sight of sand and tree
Like one deep spell-bound did he seem to be,

And moved by some strange phantasy; his eyes
Were wide distended as in glad surprise
At something there he saw; his arms reached
    o'er
The vessel's side as if to greet the shore,
And sounds came from his lips like sobs of joy.

A brief time so; and then the blue-eyed boy
Sank down convulsed, as if to him appeared
Strange sights that they saw not; and all afeard
Grew the late joyous people with vague dread;
And loud the mother wailed above her dead.

The ship steered in and found a bay, and then
The anchor plunged aweary-like: the men
Breathed breaths of rest at treading land agen.

Upon the beach by Christian men untrod
The wanderers kneeling offered up to God
The land's first-fruits; and nigh the kneeling band
The burdened mother sat upon the sand,
And still she wailed, not praying.

'Neath the wood
That lined the beach a crowd of watchers stood:
Tall men spear-armed, with skins like dusky night,
And aspect blended of deep awe and fright.
The ship that morn they saw, like some vast bird,
Come sailing toward their country; and they heard
The voices now of those strange men whose eyes
Were turned aloft, who spake unto the skies!

They heard and feared, not knowing, that **first**
    prayer,
But feared not when the wail arose, for there
Was some familiar thing did not appall, —
Grief, common heritage and lot of all.
They moved and breathed more freely at the **cry,**
And slowly from the wood, and timorously,
They one by one emerged upon the beach.
The white men saw, and like to friends did reach
Their hands unarmed; and soon the dusky crowd
Drew nigh and stood where wailed the mother
    loud.
They claimed her kindred, they could understand

That woe was hers and theirs ; whereas the band
Of white-skinned men did not as brethren seem.

But now, behold! a man, whom one would deem
From eye and mien, wherever met, a King,
Did stand beside the woman.   No youth's spring
Was in the foot that naked pressed the sand ;
No warrior's might was in the long dark hand
That waved his people backward ; no bright gold
Of lace or armor glittered ; gaunt and old, —
A belt, half apron, made of emu-down,
Upon his loins ; upon his head no crown
Save only that which eighty years did trace
In whitened hair above his furrowed face.
Nigh nude he was : a short fur boka hung
In toga-folds upon his back, but flung
From his right arm and shoulder, — ever there
The spear-arm of the warrior is bare.

So stood he nigh the woman, gaunt and wild
But king-like, spearless, looking on the child
That lay with livid face upon her knees.

Thus long and fixed he gazed, as one who sees
A symbol hidden in a simple thing,
And trembles at its meaning: so the King
Fell trembling there, and from his breast there
    broke
A cry, part joy, part fear; then to his folk
With upraised hands he spoke one guttural word,
And said it over thrice; and when they heard,
They, too, were stricken with strange fear and joy.

The white-haired King then to the breathless boy
Drew closer still, while all the dusky crowd
In weird abasement to the earth were bowed.
Across his breast the aged ruler wore
A leathern thong or belt; whate'er it bore
Was hidden 'neath the boka. As he drew
Anigh the mother, from his side he threw
Far back the skin that made his rich-furred robe,
And showed upon the belt a small red globe
Of carven wood, bright-polished, as with years:
When this they saw, deep grew his people's fears,
And to the white sand were their foreheads
    pressed.

The King then raised his arms, as if he blest
The youth who lay there seeming dead and cold;
Then took the globe and oped it, and behold!
Within it, bedded in the carven case,
There lay a precious thing for that rude race
To hold, though it as God they seemed to prize, —
A Pearl of purest hue and wondrous size!

And as the sunbeams kissed it, from the dead
The dusk King looked, and o'er his snowy head
With both long hands he raised the enthroned
        gem,
And turned him toward the strangers: e'en on
        them
Before the lovely Thing, an awe did fall
To see that worship deep and mystical,
That King with upraised god, like rev'rent priest
With elevated Host at Christian feast.

Then to the mother turning slow, the King
Took out the Pearl, and laid the beauteous Thing
Upon the dead boy's mouth and brow and breast,

And as it touched him, lo! the awful rest
Of death was broken, and the youth uprose!

.   .   .   .   .   .

Nine years passed over since on that fair shore
The wanderers knelt, — but wanderers they **no**
    more.
With hopeful hearts they bore the promise-pain
Of early labor, and soon bending grain
And herds and homesteads and a teeming **soil**
A thousand-fold repaid their patient toil.

Nine times the sun's high glory glared above,
As if his might set naught on human love,
But yearned to scorn and scorch the things **that**
    grew
On man's poor home, till all the forest's hue
Of blessed green was burned to dusty brown;
And still the ruthless rays rained fiercely **down,**
Till insects, reptiles, shrivelled as they lay,
And piteous cracks, like lips, in parching clay
Sent silent pleadings skyward, — as if she,

The fruitful, generous mother, plaintively
Did wail for water.   Lo! her cry is heard,
And swift, obedient to the Ruler's word,
From Southern iceland sweeps the cool sea breeze,
To fan the earth and bless the suffering trees,
And bear dense clouds with bursting weight of
    rain
To soothe with moisture all the parching pain.

Oh, Mercy's sweetest symbol! only they
Who see the earth agape in burning day,
Who watch its living things thirst-stricken lie,
And turn from brazen heaven as they die, —
Their hearts alone, the shadowy cloud can prize
That veils the sun, — as to poor earth-dimmed eyes
The sorrow comes to veil our joy's dear face,
All rich in mercy and in God's sweet grace!

Thrice welcome, clouds from seaward, settling down
O'er thirsting nature!   Now the trees' dull brown
Is washed away, and leaflet buds appear,
And youngling undergrowth, and far and near

The bush is whispering in her pent-up glee,
As myriad roots bestir them to be free,
And drink the soaking moisture; while brignt
    heaven
Shows clear, as inland are the spent clouds driven ,
And oh! that arch, that sky's intensate hue!
That deep, God-painted, unimagined blue
Through which the golden sun now smiling sails,
And sends his love to fructify the vales
That late he seemed to curse! Earth throbs and
    heaves
With pregnant prescience of life and leaves;
The shadows darken 'neath the tall trees' screen,
While round their stems the rank and velvet green
Of undergrowth is deeper still; and there,
Within the double shade and steaming air,
The scarlet palm has fixed its noxious root,
And hangs the glorious poison of its fruit;
And there, 'mid shaded green and shaded light,
The steel-blue silent birds take rapid flight
From earth to tree and tree to earth; and there
The crimson-plumaged parrot cleaves the air

Like flying fire, and huge brown owls awake
To watch, far down, the stealing carpet snake,
Fresh-skinned and glowing in his changing **dyes,**
With evil wisdom in the cruel eyes
That glint like gems as o'er his head flits by
The blue-black armor of the emperor-fly;
And all the humid earth displays its powers
Of prayer, with incense from the hearts of **flowers**
That load the air with beauty and with **wine**
Of mingled color, as with one design
Of making there a carpet to be trod,
In woven splendor, by the feet of God !

And high o'erhead is color: round and **round**
The towering gums and tuads, closely **wound**
Like cables, creep the climbers to the sun,
And over all the reaching branches run
And hang, and still send shoots that climb **and**
    wind
Till every arm and spray and leaf is twined,
And miles of trees, like brethren joined in love,
Are drawn and laced; while round them and
    above,

When all is knit, the creeper rests for days
As gathering might, and then one blinding blaze
Of very glory sends, in wealth and strength,
Of scarlet flowers o'er the forest's length!

Such scenes as these have subtile power to trace
Their clear-lined impress on the mind and face;
And these strange simple folk, not knowing why,
Grew more and more to silence; and the eye,
The quiet eye of Swedish gray, grew deep
With listening to the solemn rustling sweep
From wings of Silence, and the earth's great psalm
Intoned forever by the forest's calm.

But most of all was younger Jacob changed:
From morn till night, alone, the woods he ranged,
To kindred, pastime, sympathy estranged.
Since that first day of landing from the ship
When with the Pearl on brow and breast and lip
The aged King had touched him and he rose,
His former life had left him, and he chose
The woods as home, the wild, uncultured men
As friends and comrades. It were better then,

His brethren said, the boy had truly died
*Than they should live to be by him denied,
As now they were.   He lived in sombre mood,
He spoke no word to them, he broke no food
That they did eat: his former life was dead, —
The soul brought back was not the soul that
     fled !
'Twas Jacob's form and feature, but the light
Within his eyes was strange unto their sight.

His mother's grief was piteous to see :
Unloving was he to the rest, but she
Held undespairing hope that deep within
Her son's changed heart was love that she might
     win
By patient tenderness ; and so she strove
For nine long years, but won no look of love !

At last his brethren gazed on him with awe,
And knew untold that from the form they saw
Their brother's gentle mind was sure dispelled,
And now a gloomy savage soul it held.

From that first day, close intercourse he had
With those who raised him up, — fierce men,
    unclad,
Spear-armed and wild, in all their ways uncouth,
And strange to every habit of his youth.
His food they brought, his will they seemed to
    crave,
The wildest bushman tended like a slave ;
He worked their charms, their hideous chants he
    sung ;
Though dumb to all his own, their guttural tongue
He often spoke in tones of curt command,
And kinged it proudly o'er the dusky band.

And once each year there gathered from afar
A swarming host, as if a sudden war
Had called them forth, and with them did they
    bring
In solemn, savage pomp the white-haired King,
Who year by year more withered was and weak ;
And he would lead the youth apart and speak

Some occult words, and from the carven case
Would take the Pearl and touch the young man's
    face,
And hold it o'er him blessing; while the crowd,
As on the shore, in dumb abasement bowed.
And when the King had closed the formal rite,
The rest held savage revelry by night,
Round blazing fires, with dance and orgies base,
That roused the sleeping echoes of the place,
Which down the forest vistas moaned the din,
Like spirits pure beholding impious sin.

Nine times they gathered thus; but on the last
The old king's waning life seemed well-nigh past.
His feeble strength had failed: he walked no
    more,
But on a woven spear-wood couch they bore
With careful tread the form that barely gasped,
As if the door of death now hung unhasped,
Awaiting but a breath to swing, and show
The dim eternal plain that stretched below.

The tenth year waned: the cloistered bush **was**
    stilled,
The earth lay sleeping, while the clouds distilled
In ghostly veil their blessing.   Thin and white,
Through opening trees the moonbeams cleft **the**
    night,
And showed the sombre arches, taller far
Than grandest aisles of built cathedrals are.
And up those dim-lit aisles in silence streamed
Tall men with trailing spears, until it seemed,
So many lines converged of endless length,
A nation there was gathered in its strength.

Around one spot was kept a spacious ring,
Where lay the body of the white-haired **King,**
Which all the spearmen gathered to behold
Upon its spear-wood litter, stiff and cold.
All naked, there the dusky corse was laid
Beneath a royal tuad's mourning shade ;
Upon the breast was placed the carven **case**
That held the symbol of their ancient **race,**

And eyes awe-stricken saw the mystic Thing
That soon would clothe another as their King!
The midnight moon was high and white o'erhead,
And threw a ghastly pallor round the dead
That heightened still the savage pomp and state
In which they stood expectant, as for Fate
To move and mark with undisputed hand
The one amongst them to the high command.
And long they stood unanswered; each on each
Had looked in vain for motion or for speech:
Unmoved as ebon statues, grand and tall,
They ringed the shadowy circle, silent all.

Then came a creeping tremor, as a breeze
With cooling rustle moves the summer trees
Before the thunder crashes on the ear;
The dense ranks turn expectant, as they hear
A sound, at first afar, but nearing fast;
The outer crowd divides, as waves are cast
On either side a tall ship's cleaving bow,
Or mould is parted by the fearless plough
That leaves behind a passage clear and broad:

So through the murmuring multitude a road
Was cleft with power, up which in haughty swing
A figure stalking broke the sacred ring,
And stood beside the body of the King!

'Twas Jacob Eibsen, sad and gloomy-browed,
Who bared his neck and breast, one **moment**
    bowed
Above the corse, and then stood proud and tall,
And held the carven case before them all!
A breath went upward like a smothered fright
From every heart, to see that face, so white,
So foreign to their own, but marked with **might**
From source unquestioned, and to them divine;
Whilst he, the master of the mystic sign,
Then oped the case and took the Pearl and raised,
As erst the King had done, and upward **gazed**,
As swearing fealty to God on high!

But ere the oath took form, there thrilled a **cry**
Of shivering horror through the hush of night;
And there before him, blinded by the sight

Of all his impious purpose, brave with love,
His mother stood, and stretched her arms above
To tear the idol from her darling's hand ;
But one fierce look, and rang a harsh command
In Jacob's voice, that smote her like a sword.
A thousand men sprang forward at the word,
To tear the mother from the form of stone,
And cast her forth ; but, as he stood alone,
The keen, heart-broken wail that cut the air
Went two-edged through him, half reproach, half
  prayer.

But all unheeding, he nor marked her cry
By sign or look within the gloomy eye ;
But round his body bound the carven case,
And swore the fealty with marble face.

As fades a dream before slow-waking sense,
The shadowy host, that late stood fixed and dense,
Began to melt; and as they came erewhile,
The streams flowed backward through each moon-
  lit aisle ;

And soon he stood alone within the place,
Their new-made king, — their king with pallid face,
Their king with strange foreboding and unrest,
And half-formed thoughts, like dreams, within his
    breast.
Like Moses' rod, that mother's cry of woe
Had struck for water; but the fitful flow
That weakly welled and streamed did seem to
    mock
Before it died forever on the rock.

The sun rose o'er the forest, and his light
Made still more dreamlike all the evil night.
Day streamed his glory down the aisles' dim arch,
All hushed and shadowy like a pillared church;
And through the lonely bush no living thing
Was seen, save now and then a garish wing
Of bird low-flying on its silent way.

But woful searchers spent the weary day
In anxious dread, and found not what they
    sought, —

Their mother and their brother: evening brought
A son and father to the lonesome place
That saw the last night's scene ; and there, her face
Laid earthward, speaking dumbly to her heart,
They found her, as the hands that tore apart
The son and mother flung her from their chief,
And with one cry her heart had spent its grief.

They bore the cold earth that so late did move
In household happiness and works of love,
Unto their rude home, lonely now ; and he
Who laid her there, from present misery
Did turn away, half-blinded by his tears,
To see with inward eye the far-off years
When Swedish toil was light and hedgerows
    sweet ;
Where, when the toil was o'er, he used to meet
A simple gray-eyed girl, with sun-browned face,
Whose love had won his heart, and whose sweet
    grace
Had blessed for threescore years his humble life.

So Jacob Eibsen mourned his faithful wife,
And found the world no home when she was gone.
The days that seemed of old to hurry on
Now dragged their course, and marred the wish
    that grew,
When first he saw her grave, to sleep there too.
But though to him, whose yearning hope outran
The steady motion of the seasons' plan,
The years were slow in coming, still their pace
With awful sureness left a solemn trace,
Like dust that settles on an open page,
On Jacob Eibsen's head, bent down with age ;
And ere twice more the soothing rains had come,
The old man had his wish, and to his home,
Beneath the strange trees' shadow where she lay,
They bore the rude-made bier ; and from that day,
When round the parent graves the brethren stood,
Their new-made homesteads were no longer good,
But marked they seemed by some o'erhanging
    dread
That linked the living with the dreamless dead.

Grown silent with the woods the men were all,
But words were needed not to note the pall
That each one knew hung o'er them. Duties
     now,
With straying herds or swinging scythe, or plough,
Were cheerless tasks : like men they were who
     wrought
A weary toil that no repayment brought.
And when the seasons came and went, and still
The pall was hanging o'er them, with one will
They yoked their oxen teams and piled the loads
Of gear selected for the aimless roads
That nature opens through the bush ; and when
The train was ready, women-folk and men
Went over to the graves and wept and prayed,
Then rose and turned away, but still delayed
Ere leaving there forever those poor mounds.

The next bright sunrise heard the teamsters'
     sounds
Of voice and whip a long day's march away ;
And wider still the space grew day by day

From their old resting-place : the trackless wood
Still led them on with promises of good,
As when the mirage leads a thirsty band
With palm-tree visions o'er the arid sand.

I know not where they settled down at last :
Their lives and homes from out my tale have
      passed,
And left me naught, or seeming naught, to trace
But cheerless record of the empty place,
Where long unseen the palm-thatched cabins stood,
And made more lonely still the lonesome wood.

Long lives of men passed over ; but the years,
That line men's faces with hard cares and tears,
Pass lightly o'er a forest, leaving there
No wreck of young disease or old despair ;
For trees are mightier than men, and Time,
When left by cunning Sin and dark-browed
      Crime
To work alone, hath ever gentle mood.
Unchanged the pillars and the arches stood,

But shadowed taller vistas ; and the earth,
That takes and gives the ceaseless death and birth,
Was blooming still, as once it bloomed before
When sea-tired eyes beheld the beauteous shore.

But man's best work is weak, nor stands nor
    grows
Like Nature's simplest. Every breeze that blows,
Health-bearing to the forest, plays its part
In hasting graveward all his humble art.

Beneath the trees the cabins still remained,
By all the changing seasons seared and stained ;
Grown old and weirdlike, as the folk might grow
In such a place, who left them long ago.

Men came, and wondering found the work of
    men
Where they had deemed them first. The savage
    then
Heard through the wood the axe's deathwatch
    stroke
For him and all his people : odorous smoke

Of burning sandal rose where white men dwelt,
Around the huts ; but they had shuddering felt
The weird, forbidden aspect of the spot,
And left the place untouched to mould and rot.
The woods grew blithe with labor : all around,
From point to point, was heard the hollow sound,
The solemn, far-off clicking on the ear
That marks the presence of the pioneer.
And children came like flowers to bless the toil
That reaped rich fruitage from the virgin soil ;
And through the woods they wandered fresh **and**
    fair,
To feast on all the beauties blooming there.
But always did they shun the spot where grew,
From earth once tilled, the flowers of rarest hue.
There wheat grown wild in rank luxuriance
    spread,
And fruits grown native ; but a sudden tread
Or bramble's fall would foul goanos wake,
Or start the chilling rustle of the snake ;
And diamond eyes of these and thousand more,
Gleamed out from ruined roof and wall and floor.

The new-come people, they whose axes rung
Throughout the forest, spoke the English tongue,
And never knew that men of other race
From Europe's fields had settled in the place ;
But deemed these huts were built some long-past
    day
By lonely seamen who were cast away
And thrown upon the coast, who there had built
Their homes, and lived until some woe or guilt
Was bred among them, and they fled the sight
Of scenes that held a horror to the light.

But while they thought such things, the spell that
    hung,
And cast its shadow o'er the place, was strung
To utmost tension that a breath would break,
And show between the rifts the deep blue lake
Of blessed peace, — as next to sorrow lies
A stretch of rest, rewarding hopeful eyes.
And while such things bethought this new-come
    folk,
That breath was breathed, the olden spell was
    broke :

From far away within the unknown land,
O'er belts of forest and o'er wastes of sand,
A cry came thrilling, like a cry of pain
From suffering heart and half-awakened brain ;
As one thought dead who wakes within the tomb,
And, reaching, cries for sunshine in the gloom.

In that strange country's heart, whence comes the
    breath
Of hot disease and pestilential death,
Lie leagues of wooded swamp, that from the hills
Seem stretching meadows ; but the flood that fills
Those valley-basins has the hue of ink,
And dismal doorways open on the brink,
Beneath the gnarlèd arms of trees that grow
All leafless to the top, from roots below
The Lethe flood ; and he who enters there
Beneath their screen sees rising, ghastly-bare,
Like mammoth bones within a charnel dark,
The white and ragged stems of paper-bark,
That drip down moisture with a ceaseless drip,
From lines that run like cordage of a ship :

For myriad creepers struggle to the light,

And twine and mat o'erhead in murderous
    fight

For life and sunshine, like another race

That wars on brethren for the highest place.

Between the water and the matted screen,

The baldhead vultures, two and two, are seen

In dismal grandeur, with revolting face

Of foul grotesque, like spirits of the place ;

And now and then a spear-shaped wave goes by,

Its apex glittering with an evil eye

That sets above its enemy and prey,

As from the wave in treacherous, slimy way

The black snake winds, and strikes the bestial bird,

Whose shriek-like wailing on the hills is heard.

Beyond this circling swamp, a circling waste

Of baked and barren desert land is placed, —

A land of awful grayness, wild and stark,

Where man will never leave a deeper mark,

On leagues of fissured clay and scorching stones,

Than may be printed there by bleaching bones.

Within this belt, that keeps a savage guard,
As round a treasure sleeps a dragon ward,
A forest stretches far of precious trees ;
Whence came, one day, an odor-laden breeze
Of jam-wood bruised, and sandal sweet in smoke.
For there long dwelt a numerous native folk
In that heart-garden of the continent, —
There human lives with aims and fears were
    spent,
And marked by love and hate and peace and pain,
And hearts well-filled and hearts athirst for gain,
And lips that clung, and faces bowed in shame ;
For, wild or polished, man is still the same,
And loves and hates and envies in the wood,
With spear and boka and with manners rude,
As loves and hates his brother shorn and sleek,
Who learns by lifelong practice how to speak
With oily tongue, while in his heart below
Lies rankling poison that he dare not show.

Afar from all new ways this people dwelt,
And knew no books, and to no God had knelt,

And had no codes to rule them writ in blood;
But savage, selfish, nomad-lived and rude,
With human passions fierce from unrestraint,
And free as their loose limbs; with every taint
That earth can give to that which God has given;
Their nearest glimpse of Him, o'er-arching heaven,
Where dwelt the giver and preserver, — Light,
Who daily slew and still was slain by Night.

A savage people they, and prone to strife;
Yet men grown weak with years had spent a life
Of peace unbroken, and their sires, long dead,
Had equal lives of peace unbroken led.
It was no statute's bond or coward fear
Of retribution kept the shivering spear
In all those years from fratricidal sheath;
But one it was who ruled them, — one whom
        Death
Had passed as if he saw not, — one whose word
Through all that lovely central land was heard
And bowed to, as of yore the people bent,
In desert wanderings, to a leader sent

To guide and guard them to a promised land.
O'er all the Austral tribes he held command, —
A man unlike them and not of their race,
A man of flowing hair and pallid face,
A man who strove by no deft juggler's art
To keep his kingdom in the people's heart,
Nor held his place by feats of brutal might
Or showy skill, to please the savage sight;
But one who ruled them as a King of kings,
A man above, not of them, — one who brings,
To prove his kingship to the low and high,
The inborn power of the regal eye!

Like him of Sinai with the stones of law,
Whose people almost worshipped when they saw
The veiled face whereon God's glory burned;
But yet who, mutable as water, turned
From that veiled ruler who had talked with God,
To make themselves an idol from a clod:
So turned one day this savage Austral race
Against their monarch with the pallid face.
The young men knew him not, the old had heard
In far-off days, from men grown old, a word

That dimly lighted up the mystic choice
Of this their alien King, — how once a voice
Was heard by their own monarch calling clear,
And leading onward, where as on a bier
A dead child lay upon a woman's knees ;
Whom when the old King saw, like one who sees
Far through the mist of common life, he spoke
And touched him with the Pearl, and he awoke,
And from that day the people owned his right
To wear the Pearl and rule them, when the light
Had left their old King's eyes. But now, they said,
The men who owned that right were too long
    dead ;
And they were young and strong and held their
    spears
In idle resting through this white King's fears,
Who still would live to rule them till they changed
Their men to puling women, and estranged
To Austral hands the spear and coila grew.

And so they rose against him, and they slew
The white-haired men who raised their hands to
    warn,

And true to ancient trust in warning fell,
While o'er them rang the fierce revolters' yell.
Then midst the dead uprose the King in scorn,
Like some strong, hunted thing that stands at
    bay
To win a brief but desperate delay.
A moment thus, and those within the ring
'Gan backward press from their unarmèd King,
Who swept his hand as though he bade them fly,
And brave no more the anger of his eye.
The heaving crowd grew still before that face,
And watched him take the ancient carven case,
And ope it there, and take the Pearl and stand
As once before he stood, with upraised hand
And upturned eyes of inward worshipping.

Awe-struck and dumb, once more they owned him
    King,
And humbly crouched before him ; when a sound,
A whirring sound that thrilled them, passed o'er-
    head,
And with a spring they rose : a spear had sped

With aim unerring and with deathful might,
And split the awful centre of their sight, —
The upraised Pearl!   A moment there it shone
Before the spear-point, — then forever gone !

.   .   .   .   .

The spell that long the ruined huts did shroud
Was rent and scattered, as a hanging cloud
In moveless air is torn and blown away
By sudden gust uprising ; and one day
When evening's lengthened shadows came to **hush**
The children's voices, and the awful bush
Was lapt in sombre stillness, and on high
Above the arches stretched the frescoed sky, —
When all the scene such chilling aspect wore
As marked one other night long years before,
When through the reaching trees the moonlight
    shone
Upon a prostrate form, and o'er it one
With kingly gesture.   Now the light is shed
No more on youthful brow and daring head,

But on a man grown weirdly old, whose face
Keeps turning ever to some new-found place
That rises up before him like a dream ;
And not unlike a dreamer does he seem,
Who might have slept, unheeding time's sure
    flow,
And woke to find a world he does not know.
His long white hair flows o'er a form low bowed
By wondrous weight of years : he speaks aloud
In garbled Swedish words, with piteous wist,
As long-lost objects rise through memory's mist.
Again and once again his pace he stays,
As crowding images of other days
Loom up before him dimly, and he sees
A vague, forgotten friendship in the trees
That reach their arms in welcome ; but agen
These olden glimpses vanish, and dark men
Are round him, dumb and crouching, and Le
    stands
With guttural sentences and upraised hands,
That hold a carven case, — but empty now,
Which makes more pitiful the aged brow

Full-turned to those tall tuads that did hear
A son's fierce mandate and a mother's prayer.

Ah, God! what memories can live of these,
Save only with the half-immortal trees
That saw the death of one, the other lost?

The weird-like figure now the bush has crost
And stands within the ring, and turns and moans.
With arms out-reaching and heart-piercing tones,
And groping hands, as one a long time blind
Who sees a glimmering light on eye and mind.
From tree to sky he turns, from sky to earth,
And gasps as one to whom a second birth
Of wondrous meaning is an instant shown.

Who is this wreck of years, who all alone,
In savage raiment and with words unknown,
Bows down like some poor penitent who fears
The wrath of God provoked? — this man who hears
Around him now, wide circling through the wood,
The breathing stillness of a multitude?

Who catches dimly through his straining sight
The misty vision of an impious rite?
Who hears from one a cry that rends his heart,
And feels that loving arms are torn apart,
And by his mandate fiercely thrust aside?
Who is this one who crouches where she died,
With face laid earthward as her face was laid,
And prays for her as she for him once prayed?

'Tis Jacob Eibsen, Jacob Eibsen's son,
Whose occult life and mystic rule are done,
And passed away the memory from his brain.
'Tis Jacob Eibsen, who has come again
To roam the woods, and see the mournful gleams
That flash and linger of his old-time dreams.

The morning found him where he sank to rest
Within the mystic circle: on his breast
With withered hands, as to the dearest place,
He held and pressed the empty carven case.

That day he sought the dwellings of his folk;
And when he found them, once again there broke

The far-off light upon him, and he cried
From that wrecked cabin threshold for a guide
To lead him, old and weary, to his own.
And surely some kind spirit heard his moan,
And led him to the graves where they were laid.
The evening found him in the tuads' shade,
And like a child at work upon the spot
Where they were sleeping, though he knew it not.

Next day the children found him, and they gazed
In fear at first, for they were sore amazed
To see a man so old they never knew,
Whose garb was savage, and whose white hair
    grew
And flowed upon his shoulders; but their awe
Was changed to love and pity when they saw
The simple work he wrought at; and they came
And gathered flowers for him, and asked his
    name,
And laughed at his strange language; and he
    smiled
To hear them laugh, as though himself a child.

Ere that brief day was o'er, from far and near
The children gathered, wondering; and though
    fear
Of scenes a long time shunned at first restrained,
The spell was broken, and soon naught remained
But gladsome features, where of old was dearth
Of happy things and cheery sounds of mirth.
The lizards fled, the snakes and bright-eyed things
Found other homes, where childhood never sings;
And all because poor Jacob, old and wild,
White-haired and fur-clad, was himself a child.
Each day he lived amid these scenes, his ear
Heard far-off voices growing still more clear;
And that dim light that first he saw in gleams
Now left him only in his troubled dreams.

From far away the children loved to come
And play and work with Jacob at his home.
He learned their simple words with childish lip,
And told them often of a white-sailed ship
That sailed across a mighty sea, and found
A beauteous harbor, all encircled round

With flowers and tall green trees; but when they
    asked
What did the shipmen then, his mind was tasked
Beyond its strength, and Jacob shook his head,
And with them laughed, for all he knew was said

The brawny sawyers often ceased their toil,
As Jacob with the children passed, to smile
With rugged pity on their simple play;
Then, gazing after the glad group, would say
How strange it was to see that snowy hair
And time-worn figure with the children fair.

So Jacob Eibsen lived through years of joy, —
A patriarch in age, in heart a boy.
Unto the last he told them of the sea
And white-sailed ship; and ever lovingly,
Unto the end, the garden he had made
He tended daily, 'neath the tuads' shade.

But one bright morning, when the children came
And roused the echoes calling Jacob's name,

The echoes only answered back the sound.
They sought within the huts, but nothing found
Save loneliness and shadow, falling chill
On every sunny searcher : boding ill,
They tried each well-known haunt, and every
    throat
Sent far abroad the bushman's cooing note.
But all in vain their searching : twilight fell,
And sent them home their sorrowing tale to tell.
That night their elders formed a torch-lit chain
To sweep the gloomy bush ; and not in vain, —
For when the moon at midnight hung o'erhead,
The weary searchers found poor Jacob — dead !

He lay within the tuad ring, his face
Laid earthward on his hands ; and all the place
Was dim with shadow where the people stood.
And as they gathered there, the circling wood
Seemed filled with awful whisperings, and stirred
By things unseen ; and every bushman heard,
From where the corse lay plain within their sight,
A woman's heart-wail rising on the night.

For over all the darkness and the fear
That marked his life from childhood, shining clear,
An arch, like God's bright rainbow, stretched
    above,
And joined the first and last, — his mother's love

They dug a grave beneath the tuads' shade,
Where all unknown to them the bones were laid
Of Jacob's kindred ; and a prayer was said
In earnest sorrow for the unknown dead,
Round which the children grouped.

                              Upon the breast
The hands were folded in eternal rest ;
But still they held, as dearest to that place
Where life last throbbed, the empty carven case.

OPINIONS OF THE PRESS.

"SONGS FROM THE SOUTHERN SEAS.'
BY JOHN BOYLE O'REILLY.

New York Arcadian.

" Like the smell of new-mown hay, or the first breath of spring, or an unexpected kiss from well-loved lips, or any other sweet, fresh, wholesome, natural delight, is to the professional reviewer the first perusal of genuine poetry by a new writer. Not for a long time have we experienced so fresh and joyous a surprise, so perfect a literary treat, as has been given us by these fresh and glowing songs by this young and hitherto utterly unknown poet. There is something so thoroughly new and natural and lifelike, something so buoyant and wholesome and true, so much original power and boldness of touch in these songs, that we feel at once that we are in the presence of a new power in poetry. This work alone places its author head and shoulder above the rank and file of contemporary versifiers. . . . The closing passages of ' Uncle Ned's ' second tale, are in the highest degree dramatic, — thrilling the reader like the bugle-note that sounds the cry to arms. Finally, several of the poems are animated by a spirit so affectionate and pure, that we feel constrained to love their writer, offering, as they do in this respect, so marked and pleasant a contrast with too much of the so-called poetry of these modern times."

Baltimore Bulletin.

" Mr. O'Reilly is a true poet — no one can read his stirring measures and his picturesque descriptive passages without at once recognizing the true singer, and experiencing the contagion of his spirit. He soars loftily and grandly, and his song peals forth with a rare roundnesss and mellowness of tone that cheers and inspirits the hearer. His subjects belong to the open air, to new fields or untrod wilds, and they are full of healthy freshness, and the vigor of sturdy, redundant life. We hail Mr. O'Reilly with pleasure, and we demand for him the cordial recognition he deserves."

Chicago Inter-Ocean.

" We may safely say that we lay these poems down with a feeling of delight that there has come among us a true poet, who can enchant by the
vivid fire of his pictures without having recourse to a trick of words, or
the re-dressing and re-torturing of old forgotten ideas. These poems, for
the most part, are fresh and lifelike as the lyrics which led our forefathers
to deeds of glory. With scarce a line of mawkish sentiment, there is the
deep heart-feeling of a true poet. His descriptions bear the impress of
truth and the realism of personal acquaintance with the incidents described. There is the flow of Scott in his narrative power, and the fire of
Macaulay in his trumpet-toned tales of war. We are much mistaken if
this man does not in the course of a few years walk the course, and show
the world how narrative poetry should be written. He has it in him, and
genius cannot be kept under hatches. Passing over ' The Dog Guard,' a
fearful picture, we come to ' The Amber Whale.' It is impossible to
describe the intense interest that surrounds this dramatic description. A
more exciting chase could hardly be conceived, and as we stand with
bated breath, while the mate drives his lance home to the vitals, and the
boats go hissing along in the wake of the wounded monster, we seem to
behold the sea red with blood, and mark the flukes as they sweep the captain's boat into eternity. Here is a portion of the story : —

" ' Then we heard the captain's order, " Heave! " and saw the harpoon fly,
   As the whales closed in with their open jaws: a shock, and a stifled cry
   Was all that we heard; then we looked to see if the crew were still
       afloat, —
   But nothing was there save a dull red patch, and the boards of the shat-
       tered boat.

" ' But that was no time for mourning words: the other two boats came in,
   And one got fast on the quarter, and one aft the starboard fin
   Of the Amber Whale. For a minute he paused, as if he were in doubt
   As to whether 'twas best to run or fight. " Lay on! " the mate roared
       out,
   " And I'll give him a lance! " The boat shot in; and the mate, when he
       saw his chance
   Of sending it home to the vitals, four times he buried his lance.'

" We next come to ' The Dukite Snake,' a tale so simply told, so beauti-
fully sad, that the heart goes out in pity to the poor young husband in his
terrible grief. The Dukite Snake never goes alone. When one is killed
the other will follow to the confines of the earth, but he will have revenge.
Upon this fact the poet has wrought a picture so true and so dramatic that
it almost chills the blood to read a tale so cruel and so life-like. . . . Among
the remaining poems of length, we have ' The Fishermen of Wexford,' ' The
Flying Dutchman,' and ' Uncle Ned's Tales.' All are good; but the last are

simply superb. We doubt if more vivid pictures of war were ever drawn. The incidents are detailed with such lifelike force, that to any one who had ever felt the enthusiastic frenzy of battle, they bring back the sounds of the shells and the shout of advancing columns. They are lifelike as the pages of Tacitus, and stir the blood to a fever heat of warlike enthusiasm. They are strains to make soldiers."

London Athenæum.

"MR. O'REILLY is the poet of a far land. He sings of Western Australia, that poorest and loveliest of all the Australias, which has received from the mother country only her shame and her crime. Mr. O'Reilly, in a short poem, speaks of the land as 'discovered ere the fitting time,' endowed with a peerless clime, but having birds that do not sing, flowers that give no scent, and trees that do not fructify. Scenes and incidents, however, known to the author, in this perfumeless and mute land, have been reproduced by him in a series of poems of much beauty. 'The King of the Vasse,' a legend of the bush, is a weird and deeply pathetic poem, admirable alike for its conception and execution."

Atlantic Monthly.

"In a modest, well-worded prelude, the poet says: —

"'From that fair land and drear land in the South,
  Of which through years I do not cease to think,
I brought a tale, learned not by word of mouth,
  But formed by finding here one golden link
And there another; and with hands unskilled
  For such fine work, but patient of all pain
For love of it, I sought therefrom to build
  What might have been at first the goodly chain.

"'It is not golden now: my craft knows more
  Of working baser metal than of fine;
But to those fate-wrought rings of precious ore
  I add these rugged iron links of mine.'

"This is not claiming enough for himself, but the reader the more gladly does him justice because of his modesty, and perhaps it is this quality in the author which oftenest commends his book. 'The King of the Vasse' is the story of a child of the first Swedish emigrants to Australia, who lies dead in his mother's arms when they land. A native chief, coming with all his people to greet the strangers, touches the boy's forehead with a great pearl, which he keeps in a carven case or shrine, and the mighty magic of it calls him back to life, but with a savage soul, as his kindred believe; for he deserts them for the natives, over whom he rules many years, inheriting and wearing the magic pearl. At last the young men of the tribe begin to question his authority, and one of them, with a spear-thrust, destroys the great pearl. Jacob Eibsen then seems repossessed by a white man's soul, and returns to the spot long since abandoned by his kindred, and finds it occupied by English settlers, whose children's simple, childlike playmate he becomes, and remains till death. The plot is good; and it is always managed with a sober simplicity, which forms an excellent ground for some strong dramatic effects. The Australian scenery and air and natural life are everywhere summoned round the story without being forced upon the reader. Here, for instance, is a picture at once vivid and intelligible, — which is not always the case with the vivid pictures of the word-painters. After the rains begin in that southern climate, —

> " ' Earth throbs and heaves
> With pregnant prescience of life and leaves;
> The shadows darken 'neath the tall trees' screen.
> While round their stems the rank and velvet green
> Of undergrowth is deeper still; and there,
> Within the double shade and steaming air,
> The scarlet palm has fixed its noxious root,
> And hangs the glorious poison of its fruit;
> And there, 'mid shaded green and shaded light,
> The steel-blue silent birds take rapid flight
> From earth to tree and tree to earth; and there
> The crimson-plumaged parrot cleaves the air
> Like flying fire, and huge brown owls awake
> To watch, far down, the stealing carpet-snake,
> Fresh-skinned and glowing in his changing dyes,
> With evil wisdom in the cruel eyes
> That glint like gems as o'er his head flits by
> The blue-black armor of the emperor-fly;
> And all the humid earth displays its powers
> Of prayer, with incense from the hearts of flowers
> That load the air with beauty and with wine
> Of mingled color. . . .

> " ' And high o'erhead is color: round and round
> The towering gums and tuads, closely wound
> Like cables, creep the climbers to the sun,
> And over all the reaching branches run
> And hang, and still send shoots that climb and wind
> Till every arm and spray and leaf is twined,
> And miles of trees, like brethren joined in love,
> Are drawn and laced; while round them and above,
> When all is knit, the creeper rests for days
> As gathering might, and then one blinding blaze
> Of very glory sends, in wealth and strength,
> Of scarlet flowers o'er the forest's length!'

" 'There are deep springs of familiar feeling (as the mother's grief for the estrangement of her savage-hearted son) also touched in this poem, in which there is due artistic sense and enjoyment of the weirdness of the motive; and, in short, we could imagine ourselves recurring more than once to the story, and liking it better and better. 'The Dog Guard' is the next best story in the book; — a horrible fact, treated with tragic realism, and skilfully kept from being merely horrible. . . . Some of the best poems in the book are the preludes to the stories."

Boston Advertiser.

" The first, and in many respects the best poem in the book, is ' The King of the Vasse,' which is a story of the very earliest settlement of Australia by Europeans, and before a convict settlement was established there. There is to it far greater care and finish than to any of the other long poems. In some parts it is weird and strange to a degree; in others it is pathetic, — everywhere it is simple, with a pleasant flow of rhythm, and closely true to nature. It is followed by ' The Dog Guard,' a poem which leaves an impression on the mind like Coleridge's 'Ancient Mariner'— a subject which, but for great skill in the treatment, would have been repulsive. As it stands in the book it shows eminent descriptive power, and a certain freedom and daring that lifts it far above the commonplace. Interspersed among the longer poems are short verses, which must answer the same purpose in the book as the organist's interludes, helping out the value of that which precedes, and that which follows. Some of these are more than excellent. They stand out as a peculiar feature of the book, adding to its completeness, as they will add to the poet's reputation. Preceding ' The Dog Guard ' we have the following, which perhaps is as characteristic as any of the preludes. It will be seen that the burden of this, as indeed of the whole book, is Western Australia: —

> " ' Nation of Sun and Sin,
> Thy flowers and crimes are red,
> And thy heart is sore within
> While the glory crowns thy head.
> Land of the songless birds,
> What was thine ancient crime,
> Burning through lapse of time
> Like a prophet's cursing words?

> " ' Aloes and myrrh and tears
> Mix in thy bitter wine:
> Drink, while the cup is thine
> Drink, for the draught is sign
> Of thy reign in coming years.'

" Mr. O'Reilly has done his work faithfully and well; he has given us in his book more than he promised us in the preface; and to-day, with his first poetical venture before the public, he has added another to the laurels he has already won in other fields."

New York Tribune.

"These songs are the most stirring tales of adventure imaginable, chiefly placed in Western Australia, a penal colony, which has ' received from the mother country only her shame and her crime.' The book is the very melodrama of poetry. . . . Mr. O'Reilly is a man whose career has been full of wild and varied adventure, and who has put these stirring scenes — all of which he saw, and part of which he was — into verse as spontaneous and unconventional as the life he describes. His rhymed tales are as exciting as ghost stories, and we have been reading them while the early sullen November night closed in, with something the same feeling, the queer shiver of breathless expectation, with which we used to listen to legends of ghosts and goblins by our grandmother's firelight. Not that the supernatural figures too largely in these tales, — the actors in them are far more formidable than any disembodied spirits. . . . ' The King of the Vasse' is a wonderful story, in which a dead child is raised to life by a pagan incantation and the touch of a mystic pearl on the face, — which will charm the lovers of the miraculous. 'The Amber Whale,' 'The Dog Guard,' and 'Haunted by Tigers,' are in the same vein with 'The Monster Diamond.' Thrilling tales all of them. 'Chunder Ali's Wife ' is a charming little Oriental love story; a ' Legend of the Blessed Virgin' is full of tenderness and grace, for Mr. O'Reilly is both a Catholic and an Irishman; and I cannot close my extracts from his book more fittingly than with his heartfelt lines to his ' Native Land ':—

> " ' It chanced to me upon a time to sail
>   Across the Southern Ocean to and fro;
> And, landing at fair isles, by stream and vale
>   Of sensuous blessing did we ofttimes go.
> And months of dreamy joys, like joys in sleep,
>   Or like a clear, calm stream o'er mossy stone,
> Unnoted passed our hearts with voiceless sweep,
>   And left us yearning still for lands unknown.

> " ' And when we found one, — for 'tis soon to find
>   In thousand-isled Cathay another isle, —
> For one short noon its treasures filled the mind,
>   And then again we yearned, and ceased to smile.
> And so it was, from isle to isle we passed,
>   Like wanton bees or boys on flowers or lips;
> And when that all was tasted, then at last
>   We thirsted still for draughts instead of sips.

> " ' I learned from this there is no Southern land
>   Can fill with love the hearts of Northern men.
> Sick minds need change; but, when in health they **stand**
>   'Neath foreign skies their love flies home again.

And thus with me it was: the yearning turned
 From laden airs of cinnamon away,
And stretched far westward, while the full heart burned
 With love for Ireland, looking on Cathay!

" ' My first dear love, all dearer for thy grief!
 My land that has no peer in all the sea
For verdure, vale, or river, flower or leaf, —
 It first to no man else, thou'rt first to me.
New loves may come with duties, but the first
 Is deepest yet, — the mother's breath and smiles :
Like that kind face and breast where I was nursed
 Is my poor land, the Niobe of isles.' "

Mr. R. H. Stoddard, in Scribner's Monthly.

" ' The King of the Vasse,' the opening poem in Mr. O'Reilly's volume,
is a remarkable one; and if the legend be the creation of Mr. O'Reilly, it
places him high among the few really imaginative poets. . . . This, in brief,
is the outline of the ' King of the Vasse.' In it we could point out many
faulty lines. William Morris could have spun off the verse more fluently,
and Longfellow could have imparted to it his usual grace. Still, we are
glad that it is not from them, but from Mr. O'Reilly, that we receive
it. The story is simply and strongly told, and is imaginative and
pathetic. It is certainly the most poetic poem in the volume, though by
no means the most striking one. ' The Amber Whale ' is more characteristic of Mr. O'Reilly's genius, as ' The Dog Guard ' and ' The Dukite
Snake ' are more characteristic of the region in which he is most at home.
. . . . He is as good a balladist as Walter Thornbury, who is the
only other living poet who could have written ' The Old Dragoon's
Story.' "

Boston Gazette.

" This is a volume of admirable poetry. The more ambitious poems in
the book are in narrative form, and are terse and spirited in style, and full
of dramatic power and effect. Mr. O'Reilly is both picturesque and epi-
grammatic, and writes with a manly straightforwardness that is very
attractive. . . . Of the sickly sentimentality that forms the groundwork
of so much of our modern poetry, not a trace is to be found in this book.
The tone throughout is healthy, earnest, and pure. There is also an inde-
pendence and originality of thought and treatment that are very striking,
and which prove not the least attractive features of the book. Some of
the stories are conceived with unusual power, and are developed with
scarcely less effect and skill."

Boston Times.

"Some reminiscences of his romantic life, the poet has woven into the verses that fill this volume. Very grim reminiscences they are, of crime and death and horrors dire; but they represent faithfully, we have no doubt, the society, or rather savagery, of those far and fearsome lands. Most of the poems are stories, sombre in substance, but told with a vehement vigor that is singularly harmonious with their themes. The opening poem, 'The King of the Vasse,' preserves a strange and pathetic legend, which the poet has wrought into a powerful, but most painful story. His imagination revels in pictures of weird desolation and the repulsive and appalling prodigies of animal and vegetable life in the tropic world; and the effect of these presented in quick succession, and varied only by episodes of human sin or suffering, is positively depressing. Such passages as this abound in the poem: —

"'In that strange country's heart, whence comes the breath
Of hot disease and pestilential death,
Lie leagues of wooded swamp, that from the hills
Seem stretching meadows; but the flood that fills
These valley basins has the hue of ink
And dismal doorways open on the brink,
Beneath the gnarled arms of trees that grow
All leafless to the top, from roots below
The Lethe flood; and he who enters there
Beneath this screen sees rising, ghastly bare,
Like mammoth bones within a charnel dark,
The white and ragged stems of paper-bark,
That drip down moisture with a ceaseless drip, —
With lines that run like cordage of a ship;
For myriad creepers struggle to the light,
And twine and meet o'erhead in murderous fight
For life and sunshine. . . .

"'Between the water and the matted screen,
The bald-head vultures, two and two, are seen
In dismal grandeur, with revolting face
Of foul grotesque, like spirits of the place;
And now and then a spear-shaped wave goes by,
Its apex glittering with an evil eye
That sets above its enemy and prey
As from the wave in treacherous, slimy way
The black snake winds, and strikes the bestial bird,
Whose shriek-like wailing on the hills is heard.'

"The 'Dog Guard' is a tale of horrors. 'The Amber Whale' and 'Haunted by Tigers' are founded on whaling incidents, and the latter, especially, is eloquent with the woe of tragedy. There are a few poems in the volume written in a lighter mood. 'Uncle Ned's Tale' is a very spirited tale of battle. 'The Fishermen of Wexford' is one of the best pieces in the collection — almost severe in its simple realism, but tenderly pathetic. We have rarely seen a first volume of poems so rich in promise as is this. It is singularly free from the faults of most early poems, and exhibits a maturity of thought and a sober strength of style that would do credit to any of our older poets."

Boston Commercial Bulletin.

" His descriptive powers are remarkably strong and vivid, and his imagination powerful and vigorous. Yet it is evident from a glance at the minor poems of ' Golu,' and my ' Mother's Memory,' that the author has an imagination that will not desert him on brighter and more graceful flights of fancy. Altogether the volume is one of much more than ordinary originality and excellence."

Worcester Palladium.

" He shows originality and good descriptive power, and he treats his subjects *con amore*. . . . The author had the very best reason in the world for writing this collection, and a second volume will be awaited with reason; for strong points are displayed, and a person who writes because his heart wills it, sooner or later wins the heart of the public."

Bangor Whig.

" There is no one of the poems the book contains that has not running through it a sort of realism that at once takes possession of the reader's mind, and he looks upon it, as it were, as an actual event."

Mr. Newell (Orpheus C. Kerr) in The Catholic Review.

" Judged in all the phases of his talent presented by this book, Mr. O'Reilly is unquestionably a man of true poetic verve and temperament, with too much reverence for the noble gift of song to sophisticate it with mawkish affectations or conceited verbal ingenuities. No obscure line patches his page; no fantastic mannerism accentuates his style; no pretendedly metaphysical abstraction egotizes what he thinks worthy of gift to mankind."

Utica Herald.

" In the leading poem of Mr. O'Reilly's collection, entitled ' The King of the Vasse,' there are novelties of scene and legend which alone claim the attention. . . . The poem is in many respects a wonderful one, and contains many subtleties of thought and expression, which it is impossible to reproduce in scanty extract."

Literary World, Boston.

. . . " Mr. O'Reilly unquestionably possesses poetical talent of a high and rare order. He excels in dramatic narrative, to which his natural intensity of feeling lends a peculiar force. His verse is sometimes careless, and often lacks finish; but writers are few, nowadays, who have a better capital in heart or hand for successful poetical work than that which is evidenced in this volume."

New York Independent.

"The first and longest poem in this book, 'The King of the Vasse,' introduces us into a new country, and proves that the author's dreary Australian experiences were a gain to literature. . . . 'The Dog Guard' and 'The Amber Whale' are even better, the first being an addition of real value to our literature. Throughout the lesser poems which compose the remainder of the volume, there is such an evenness of excellence as to give good proof that the author need not confine himself to narrative poetry in order to claim an honorable place in our literature."

Chicago Times.

"This book is a striking instance that 'you find poetry nowhere unless you bring some with you.' The thousands of despairing wretches who have toiled in the chain-gangs as Mr. O'Reilly did, saw no poems in the soil which seemed to give them back the impress only of the British arrow cut on the sole of their convict shoes. But the radiant imagination and tender heart of the patriot felon found poetry on every side of him, and in his hands the driest stick becomes an Aaron's rod, and buds and blossoms. The most delightful portion of the book is its Australian legends. These reveal extraordinary dramatic power, and their rhythmical construction is perfect. Unique and incomparable, they will keep a permanent place in literature, and the romance of their origin and authorship will scarcely add anything to their beauty and completeness as poems. . . . 'Modern poets put a great deal of water in their ink,' says Goethe. O'Reilly's ink contains just water enough to keep the fluid from becoming thick. It flows like a limpid stream, flecked with clouds and sunlight, and here and there tossing with so much force into fissures of Australian rocks as to send up glittering, snowy showers of spray. O'Reilly is undoubtedly destined to reach a high place as an English poet. He is now a very young man."

Christian Era.

"As a poet, his writings have called forth admiration, and as an editor, he is worthy of great praise."

Mr. E. P. Whipple, in the Boston Globe.

" The Boston editors can boast of having a poet in their ranks, and they should naturally cherish him. . . . More than half his volume is devoted to what he saw, felt, collected, and imagined during a forced sojourn in Australia. The remaining portion consists of occasional poems, very tender, fanciful, earnest, individual, and manly, claiming nothing which they do not win by their own inherent force, grace, melody, and 'sweet reasonableness,' or it may be at times their passionate unreasonableness. Nobody can read the volume without being drawn to its author. He is so thoroughly honest and sincere that he insists that his imaginations are but memories."

New York Evening Mail.

" Most of the songs are stories of the bush or of the sea, and, strangely, the subjects are almost without exception, illustrations of the awful surety of the punishment that lays in wait for the sin of him whom men harm not — the key of Coleridge's 'Ancient Mariner.' It is almost the old Greek Fate that stalks through these tales of outlawry and wrong, and if they be indeed the legends of a convict land, they are themselves a strange showing of how crime haunts and hunts the soul. . . . Mr. O'Reilly has the natural gift of telling a story capitally, and all these tales in verse are interesting as well as powerful. He has other qualifications also as a poet; his Australian landscapes are drawn with fine artistic skill, and testify to their own truth, and about some of his pictures their is a weirdness that touches on the supernatural."

Boston Post.

" Of the author's genius in poetry the public are so well aware, through his fugitive pieces, that no commendation is necessary. His style is vigorous and manly, and combines a delicacy of sentiment with clearness of thought and vivacity of imagery. Most of these poems have a peculiar interest, from the fact that they are of a narrative form, 'relics of an unknown sphere,' of the writer's personal experience and adventure in Australia. They are uneven in merit, but by far the greater number have already taken a permanent place among the living poems of the day."

Danbury News.

" His poems, aside from their intrinsic merit and romantic interest, are worth close study, as examples of the effects produced upon the mind of a prisoner by the wild luxuriance and fantastic forms which nature assumes in Australia."

New York Tablet.

"The 'Amber Whale,' 'Dog Guard,' and 'Monster Diamond,' are among the best known of his longer poems, and they have already taken their place amongst the best narrative poems of the age. . . . We hail with very great pleasure this first collection of Mr. O'Reilly's poems, which we hope will meet with the kindly welcome it deserves from all lovers of ballad poetry."

Cincinnati Times.

"Amid the frantic strivings of modern poets to obtain a reputation for originality by wild mouthings, odd, strange, and revolting conceits, by soaring toward the empyrian, and diving into the infinite, by a false mysticism and luxuriance of verbiage, covering a poverty of ideas, it is refreshing to find one poet who is content to be original within the domain of common sense; who courts the muses, not with the freedom of a literary libertine, but modestly, yet with true poetic ardor. . . . In view of all this we take it as a most encouraging thing that such a book of poetry as 'Songs from the Southern Seas' is published, and still more encouraging its evident approval by critics and acceptableness to the public. In some of the poems, notably in 'The King of the Vasse,' there are traces of the influence of Wm. Morris, and Mr. O'Reilly could not be influenced from a sweeter, purer source; in narrative passages there is evidence of a study of Scott, and the poet could not study in this department a better model; in the war lyrics there is an evident following of the style of Macaulay, and a singer of more stirring battle-songs never lived; but throughout the book there is hardly a trace of Swinburne or the Swinburnian school. The poems are strong, earnest, and the offspring of genuine emotion. . . . Mr. O'Reilly's war lyrics, under the title of 'Uncle Ned's Tales,' are the most spirited that have been produced for a long time. They have all the ring and fire of Macaulay; they stir one's blood like the neigh of a war-horse or the blast of a bugle."

Hartford Post.

"Some of the short poems are full of thoughtful earnestness and the true poet's yearning tenderness, while seldom have more stirring lines told tales of war than those of 'Uncle Ned's Stories.' "

San Francisco Monitor.

"The volume now before us contains 'The King of the Vasse,' 'The Dog Guard,' 'The Amber Whale,' and a number of minor pieces, all of which are marked by much dramatic power and beauty of imagery, showing him to be a poet in the truest sense of the word."

Irish American.

"Originality, whether of ideas, construction, or of subjects, is the principal something invariable sought for, and but seldom found, in the generation of 'poets' with which this era of ours is so lavishly supplied. In the volume before us, however, this essential poetic quality is so strikingly manifest, that, in recognition of it, we must assign Mr. O'Reilly a very high place among the few who, in our day, write readable and meritorious verse. But this is not the only feature in Mr. O'Reilly's muse worthy of remark; the vigor of his lines, the aptness of his similes, the effectiveness of his climaxes, — all testify to the existence in the author of that true poetic disposition, which is ever inborn, and never acquired. To those who may be sceptical of our judgment, we say, read the 'Songs from the Southern Seas,' and realize the pleasure they are calculated to afford even the most critical."

Detroit Post.

"They are evidently not fictions, but faithful transcripts of his own feelings; the imagery is not stolen or borrowed, but original."

Hartford Courant.

"The volume not only contains a great deal of vigorous and interesting poetry, but it gives excellent promise for the future."

Albany Journal.

"For wild adventure and thrilling experience they will compare with the most weird and exciting legends."

Dublin Nation.

"The narratives themselves are interesting; they have usually a tragic turn, and are worked out with no small degree of skill. . . . Some of the word-pictures of Australian scenery are exceedingly realistic and vivid. . . . Some of the minor poems in this book afford much better indications of the poetic capacities of the author; and the effect of the entire volume is to lead us to believe that he has within him powers which will enable him to rise far above the mark to which he has here attained."

Lawrence American.

"There is a vein of fire and earnestness, a glow of enthusiasm, that cannot but attract to the writer, and win no slight admiration for his genius; and his countrymen will especially be pleased with the graceful volume."

Catholic Record of Philadelphia.

"It has seldom been our good fortune to discover a volume of verses in which the realistic and poetic elements were so powerfully and ably combined. Mr. O'Reilly selects his themes from among scenes and characters which would naturally be supposed to be the least congenial to the muse of song, for Erato is not usually considered at home among Nantucket tars on New Bedford whaling-ships, in Australian penal colonies, or the after-dark pranks of shameless youngsters. The luxurious arcades and flowering groves of the tropics may, indeed, be for a time her abode, and she may not disdain to occasionally bathe in the sparkling waters of sunny Southern seas, but we will stake our character for penetration on the assertion that Mr. O'Reilly is a handsome Irishman from the vicinity of Blarney Castle, for he has so completely fascinated her that she follows him with her most favoring smiles wherever or whenever he bids her presence. She is beside him in the murderer's secluded shelter; she rides with him on the storm-winds that whistle around the Horn; she sits beside him in the agonizing cruise when the wounded amber whale drags his boat through the mighty Southern spray; she perches on an oil barrel on New Bedford's wharves, or peeps with him through the windows of a New-England meeting-house. Wherever he lists, she lets him sing, — sing the tenderest of songs, and manliest of tones."

MOONDYNE:

A STORY FROM THE UNDER-WORLD.

BY JOHN BOYLE O'REILLY.

Pilot Publishing Co., Boston.   Post-free for $1.50.

OPINIONS OF THE PRESS.

From the New York Sun.

"Regarded merely with a view to its artistic merits, this is a narrative
which no lover of novels should neglect to read. Whether we look to the
strange and impressive nature of the scenery portrayed, and the abnormal
conditions of life studied — to the novelty of incident and the skilful construction of plot, or to the vigorous strokes by which the persons of the
tale are made to stand forth from the canvas — we cannot fail to recognize
in this work a strong and captivating performance. . . . We do not know
whether the author, as a matter of fact, has visited the penal colony in West
Australia, or has made a study of British prisons, but certainly his account
of convict life under these diverse conditions bears the marks of authen-
ticity. What is more to our immediate purpose, his analysis of the principles which lie at the roots of the systems of confinement and transportation,
is profound and fruitful, and his practical suggestions, enforced, as they are,
by the experience of penal settlements, where, after a certain period of
probation, the outlaws and the victims of a highly-organized society are
suffered to begin life anew, deserve to be closely scanned and maturely
pondered. . . . Such are some of the problems forced upon the reader's
attention by this remarkable book, but which are rather hinted than ex-
pounded — not so much dissected by argument as commended to our sympathies by the poignant spectacle of suffering and the winning accent of
conviction. The author seldom overlooks the limitations of his artistic
purpose, and the thread of his story may be followed with eagerness by
those who would hear with indifference the teaching of the student and the
philanthropist."

From the Chicago Times.

"*Moondyne* is remarkable in more respects than one. It has plot enough for half-a-dozen strong romances; it is written with crispness and simplicity, and in pure and nervous English; its morality is orthodox; its scene and characters are wholly novel and unique, and the interest is keenly — even painfully — sustained, . . . and no one can read *Moondyne* without loving virtue more, pitying distress, abhorring injustice, and detesting vice. It is one of the few American novels which, while intensely romantic, is lofty in its aim, eloquent and noble in its argument, and healthy and refining in its effect. It is characterized throughout by the highest dramatic intuition, and ought to find its way speedily to the boards."

From the New Orleans Morning Star and Catholic Visitor.

"This fine novel is really a treat, refined in diction, high-toned in sentiment, and instructive in details. There is no religious controversy in its pages, no tedious theological arguments in the fabric of its story, but the whole book affords its readers only pleasure and profit. The spirit which animates the work is that of philanthropy, and the dedication, 'To all who are in prison, for whatever cause,' gives the clew to the object of the writer. The characters are well drawn, although we think the hero is over-drawn — that is, he is too perfect — but as a model to youth, the exemplar must be, as far as possible, faultless. The interest of the story is splendidly sustained, and the life of 'Moondyne' is thrilling, grand, and beautiful. The lessons conveyed are very noble, and we think this expression in the mouth of Mr. Wyville, under the attendant circumstances, is the one grand lesson of the book, '*Authority must never forget humanity.*' We would like to quote several passages from the book, which for strength and pathos approach very near to the sublime — but we can only name the many striking points, and leave to the reader the pleasure of reading them in full."

From the Boston Daily Advertiser.

"Mr. O'Reilly has made a wonderful story of the convict-labor in Australia. The whole tale is on as magnificent a scale as Dumas' *Monte Cristo*, and more lofty in aim and sentiment. The vast natural wealth and bewildering beauty of the country, are made the mere setting for a group of men, who answer every demand of heroism, and for two sweet women. The villain is as bad as the heroes are good; through the whole book the interest never flags, the enthusiasm never cools, the intense dramatic and emotional power never breaks. With the same glowing ardor the eloquent author tells of superhuman courage, hair-breadth escapes, experiences in the bush, and in the convict-gangs, discusses the penal code of Australia, the responsibility of Eng and, the abstract principles of liberty and the rights of man, the origin of crime and the deepest and most tender love of man and woman. The rapid and high-wrought fiction of the story is enhanced by the rush and color of the style and the air of reality that is given to the most romantic incidents and to the wildest horrors. *Moondyne*, the title of the book, means something more than manly or kingly, and although it is applied especially to the chief god-like hero, it belongs properly to the whole group of men who are represented as lifting Australia from sin and darkness into virtue and glory by the greatness of their own souls, the strength of their own wills, and their own passion of unselfishness. And all through this gorgeous fabric runs the thread of faith in man, faith in the root of good to be found even in the worst of convicts, and in the law of kindness and encouragement, to replace in all penal colonies the law of force. Mr. O'Reilly dedicates his book 'to all who are in prison for whatever cause.' And prisoners never had a more gallant and chivalrous champion."

From the Woman's Journal.

"This book is no ordinary romance. It is the work of a man of genius, who writes a descriptive story, largely based upon his own observation and experience, colored by his own feelings, and reflecting his own opinions, aspirations, and prejudices. It could only have been written by John Boyle O'Reilly, a genuine poet and philanthropist, but also an American Catholic Irishman, an escaped Australian convict, exiled by the British Government for his participation in the Fenian insurrection. From such a man, with such an experience, it would be unfair to expect an exact picture of English or Australian life; but it is natural to expect a graphic transcript of an exceptional experience, all the more valuable because exceptional, all the more vivid because a record of scenes of which he has been an eye-witness. Australian scenery is reproduced with a wealth of word-painting which few living writers could equal. The horrible life of a penal colony is portrayed with admirable distinctness. The national and religious feelings of the writer are carefully kept in the background, and there is an evident intention of fairness all through the book."

From the Boston Traveller.

"Mr. O'Reilly has produced a strong and vigorous romance, in striking contrast with the namby-pamby literature of late offered to the public b.

exemplars of 'the great American novel.' The character of 'Moondyne' is among the noblest ever conceived by any novelist, and he who cannot read this story without attaining to a loftier inspiration toward a nobler life, who cannot sympathize with the sorrows of the sinning and down-trodden, who cannot lay it aside with a resolution to make his own life more useful and better,—such an one must be blind indeed. The author's style is not among the least attractive features of the book. Strong, yet graceful, with a certain *verve* which is delightfully invigorating, whether in giving those inimitable character sketches which mark the volume in question, or in depicting to the mind of the reader the wildness and beauty of Australian scenery, Mr. O'Reilly is equally at home. We trust that *Moondyne* will not be the last novel from his pen."

From the London Bookseller.

" A powerful and fascinating tale, illustrating different systems of treatment adopted towards criminal convicts. The story belongs to the time when Western Australia was a penal settlement, governed by laws of Draconic severity. The regulations of our prisons at home were far from satisfactory, as was proved by their frequent changes, none of which long recommended themselves to practical men. Like Jean Valjean in Victor Hugo's story, the hero of the tale under notice was a convict, who, by a turn of the wheel, rose to a position of trust, and distinguished himself as a philanthropist, and a reformer of the present system. No one who begins the story will be able to stop till it is finished."

From the Worcester Spy.

" This is a novel of harrowing and exciting description, brilliantly written, but almost too painful to allow enjoyment in the reading."

From the Boston Journal.

"There is power in the book, and pathos, and passion of a noble sort; and there is an abundance of exciting incidents and some bits of stirring and graphic description. The most jaded novel reader will find that there is something more than commonly fresh and inspiring about the story. If there are some faults of construction, and a little lack of symmetry, these are more than atoned for by the virile strength and intensity which hold the reader to the end."

From the New York Graphic.

"This brilliant and picturesque fiction obtained, as it deserved, an immediate recognition of its power and originality, and added greatly to the already enviable reputation of its versatile and gifted author. In the form in which it now appears, with its large, clear type and its attractive pages, it will increase its circle of readers, and consequently its popularity. The book is one that amply rewards the reading, not only for the fire and vigor of its style, but for the dramatic interest and the unconventionality of its plot."

From the Boston Herald.

" As a novel, we cannot but regret that the ending is so tragic, but we do not regard this volume as simply a novel. From beginning to end it is a satire upon British institutions, and we have seen nothing to surpass it since Bulwer's novel of *Paul Clifford*, where, under the guise of a love story, the author demonstrated that the prison system of England was an encouragement to crime, and that "the worst use you could put a man to was to hang him." Mr. O'Reilly's book has been favorably noticed in most of the leading journals of the country, but the Catholic newspapers criticise it very sharply, although they profess great respect for the author, and to love him sincerely. Mr. O'Reilly is not only a man of talent, but one of real genius. He is in the prime of life, and is abundantly able to take care of himself. He has written some of the best lyric poetry in the language, and although his first novel is not faultless, he has no occasion to be disturbed by any of the flies, gnats, or other dipterous insects which buzz about him."

From the Boston Post.

"Its originality is a special charm. It is full of manliness and virile power, and yet abounding in gentleness and pathos."

From the London Saturday Review.

" *Moondyne* is a really clever and graphic story of Australian life."

From the Golden Rule.

" The story is powerfully written. There is little scenic description, but Mr. O'Reilly shows a keen analysis of motives and character, and there is an imaginative glow and color suffused through the book which only the poet could impart. The book is entirely without a harlequin. There is less wit than the American reader might expect; but the interest of the story never flags, and we feel that it was omitted, not because the writer could not command it, but because he had a greater joy and confidence in the higher and more serious purposes of his book.''

From the Irish World.

"As an insight into the political and natural history of Australia alone, it is one of the most valuable books written for years past; there is so little known of that strange land of songless birds, scentless flowers, and fruitless trees so wonderfully described in Mr. O'Reilly's Australian poems. 'Moondyne,' the hero of the tale, reminds one of Victor Hugo's Jean Valjean. Body and soul ground to the dust in penal servitude for little or no crime, his grand, rough nature comes out of it unscathed by its degrading influences, and even elevated to more than human strength and beauty as he lays aside all thoughts of his own welfare, and devotes himself to the reform of the penal colony, and the amelioration of the awful slavery of his fellow-men."

From the Cambridge Tribune.

"We think the book superior to Charles Reade's book with the same object, that of calling attention to the wrongs inflicted upon convicts, and as a work of fiction it impresses one more agreeably than that."

www.ingramcontent.com/pod-product-compliance
Lightning Source LLC
Chambersburg PA
CBHW021801110726
47902CB00006B/1605